ONE ARM, ONE GUN, ONE CHANCE

Fargo climbed up through the rocks, pulling himself upward with the powerful muscles of his good arm. He looked down at the attackers. There were five of them. Some were buckskins, others were dressed in U.S. Army castoffs. The one nearest Fargo wore a belt that sported hanging pieces of dark and light fur—scalps. Maybe worse.

Fargo raised his Colt slowly. Six bullets for five men.

Fargo fired the first three shots fast, catching one in the center of the ribs, the second in the back, the third in the side of the head, exploding blood all over the fourth. The fourth tried to bring his gun around, but Fargo, shifting the aim up slightly, caught him full in the belly. The fifth managed to get his rifle full around and squeezed off a wild shot just as he took a bullet in the neck and spouted like a fountain.

Trouble was, Fargo couldn't breathe easier. He could only give a sigh. This wasn't the end of the killing—just the start, as Death Valley lived up to its name. . . .

CROWHEART'S REVENGE

THE
TRAILSMAN
151

CROWHEART'S REVENGE

by

Jon Sharpe

Ⓞ
A SIGNET BOOK

SIGNET
Published by the Penguin Group
Penguin Books USA Inc., 375 Hudson Street,
New York, New York 10014, U.S.A.
Penguin Books Ltd, 27 Wrights Lane,
London W8 5TZ, England
Penguin Books Australia Ltd, Ringwood,
Victoria, Australia
Penguin Books Canada Ltd, 10 Alcorn Avenue,
Toronto, Ontario, Canada M4V 3B2
Penguin Books (N.Z.) Ltd, 182-190 Wairau Road,
Auckland 10, New Zealand

Penguin Books Ltd, Registered Offices:
Harmondsworth, Middlesex, England

First published by Signet, an imprint of Dutton Signet,
a division of Penguin Books USA Inc.

First Printing, July, 1994
10 9 8 7 6 5 4 3 2 1

The first chapter of this book originally appeared in *Savage Guns*,
the one hundred fiftieth volume of this series.

 REGISTERED TRADEMARK—MARCA REGISTRADA

Printed in the United States of America

The Trailsman

Beginnings ... they bend the tree and they mark the man. Skye Fargo was born when he was eighteen. Terror was his midwife, vengeance his first cry. Killing spawned Skye Fargo, ruthless, cold-blooded murder. Out of the acrid smoke of gunpowder still hanging in the air, he rose, cried out a promise never forgotten.

The Trailsman they began to call him all across the West: searcher, scout, hunter, the man who could see where others only looked, his skills for hire but not his soul, the man who lived each day to the fullest, yet trailed each tomorrow. Skye Fargo, the Trailsman, the seeker who could take the wildness of a land and the wanting of a woman and make them his own.

Mojave Desert, California, 1860 . . .
a hellhole of sizzling heat and madness
where only two things could keep a man alive—
dogged duty . . . or cold-blooded revenge

1

"The answer is still no," Skye Fargo said, his voice icy. He continued to lean casually against the rough wooden wall of the colonel's office. But Fargo kept his lake blue eyes steady, locked on Colonel Power's steely gaze. A long moment passed. Then the officer glanced down at the top of his desk. The morning light, filtered through the grimy cracked windowpane, shone across the colonel's face. A muscle twitched along his jaw.

Fargo studied him. He'd met the man before, years before, in a fort on the Missouri. And now, a thousand miles west of there, they stood together again in a small room.

Colonel Darrel Power had changed. Changed a lot. His weathered cheeks were now deep-pitted and a crevice sliced the forehead between his brows. He was unbowed though, his broad shoulders set square, those of a man used to being obeyed. Tough campaigning and the scrapping life in a frontier fort would harden a man to stone, Fargo thought. Or crush him.

The colonel shifted his weight as he stood behind his desk, looking down at a stack of papers. He shifted them purposefully, his jaw working as he thought. Power glanced up again, locking eyes with Fargo.

"I can make it eight hundred dollars," he snapped. "Eight hundred and expenses."

Fargo shook his head slowly. That was a lot of money in the U.S. Army, where a sergeant drew forty greenbacks every two months.

"It's not the money," Fargo said. "I told you I've got business up in Wyoming Territory. And besides, you're not dealing straight with me. I heard two recruits talking on my way into the fort this morning. I heard there's been some newspaperman about to write how the army still can't run down the Indian renegades. These two shoetails said they'd heard you were in trouble. They'd heard your man is dead. Now, I've been around the military long enough to know that the enlisted men usually have the straight story."

The words hung in the air between them. Dust motes swirled in the shaft of sunlight awash on the wide plank floor. Colonel Power's shoulders sagged for an instant and then he turned about sharply and strode toward a map tacked on the wall.

"General Coop doesn't think the major's dead," the colonel said stiffly. "And orders are to go after him. Bring him in."

Fargo walked over to stand beside the colonel and they looked at the map together. The stained paper showed the diagonal curve of the Old Spanish Trail arcing across the vast wasteland. A large "X" on the trail marked the location of Fort Desoto, under Colonel Power's command for ten years. To the north were a few scrawls in the midst of wide blank spaces. That was where the major and his company had disappeared.

"Just west of here are the Soda Mountains," the colonel said, tracing the wavy lines with his finger. "It's an easy trail to Broken Oak's Trading Post."

"Broken Oak! Is he still around?" Fargo asked, trying to keep the amazement out of his voice. He remembered Broken Oak, the wiry half-breed trader. "What the hell's he doing out here?"

"Trading," said the colonel with a shrug. Fargo noted the tight, fake smile on his face. "They do a helluva business, so I hear. Trade with the fort all the time. If he's an old friend of yours, you might ride over and ask him about it yourself."

"Nice try," Fargo said. "The answer is still no."

The colonel ignored him and turned back to the map.

"Then come the Granite Mountains. Easy pass through there. And then you're right at a dry flat and the mouth of Rio Chingo." He ran his fingers up a sinuous line that snaked across the blank paper. "Fort Chingo is at the riverhead."

Fargo peered at the map in curiosity.

"Oh, it's not a real river," said the colonel, catching his expression. "It's a dry riverbed. Runs ten miles or so. That's why they call it Chingo. Means short. Short River, see. And there's waterholes in the riverbed. It's a real easy haul for eight hundred . . ."

"Chingo also means naked," Fargo cut in as he stepped away from the map. "Like naked rock and naked sand and naked sun broiling down. And as to waterholes. Sure. You can trudge up that river and you might find a wallow full of poison alkali water. Or you might find nothing at all."

"Eight hundred dollars."

"No."

"It's an order."

"I'm not in the army, Colonel. And just why is this major so important to you anyway?"

"General Coop's orders," Power said. "The U.S. Army always stands by its men."

Fargo glanced at the map again, his eyes traveling across the blank white spaces.

"How long has Company F been out there?"

The colonel hesitated.

"The major was sent out to establish Fort Chingo five years ago."

"Five years," Fargo repeated.

The colonel walked to his desk and rifled through the papers. He pulled out a small photograph, glanced at it momentarily, then tossed it toward Fargo.

"There he is."

Fargo picked up the tintype and held it angled against the light. In the brown reflective surface, he saw a man's face. The jaw was square and hard, the brow high and intelligent, and his light hair was long and wavy. His nose was hooked or maybe it had been broken. But the eyes were what held his attention. Deep and sunken, the major's eyes gazed out from the photograph with an electric ardor, with a look of challenge and defiance. But they were also hunted, haunted eyes.

Fargo tossed the tintype onto the desk.

"How long since they disappeared?"

Colonel Power strode away from Fargo and stood looking out the dusty window, his back to the room.

"Two."

"*Two*? Two *years*? You mean you and the U.S. Army sent a company out to the edge of hell and left them there for *two years* with no supplies? No relief? What the hell's going on?"

Above the collar of his shirt, Fargo saw the back of the colonel's neck redden.

"Drill," the colonel barked, his back still to Fargo, his voice tight with unexploded rage. "Drill. Mounting and dismounting sabre drill. Close order drill. Calls and formation." The colonel whirled about, his eyes dark. The rage built in his voice. "Drill maintains the men in fighting form. I know that. And then there are the orders. Orders from back East. Keep a hundred miles of trail clear for the settlers coming in. Keep the Indians from wreaking havoc. Mop up after the Indian agents cheat the local tribes out of land. Orders. Keep the supply lines open for the forts west. And do all that with a quarter of a regiment, five companies from the 13th Infantry. Do it with bad supplies and guns that misfire. Oh, and by the way, run down some renegades. Run down Apache devils who are on the loose. If you can spare a company or two."

The colonel whirled about, his face twitching with fury.

"So, you sent Company F."

Colonel Power clenched his jaw. His shoulders were high and tight.

"Major Conrad requested the post," said Colonel Power, slowly regaining his equilibrium. "And after we first lost contact, I sent orders for him to return. He ignored them. So I sent second orders and a troop. They never came back."

"So you left them all out there to fry," Fargo said.

He hesitated to ask the colonel another question which would make it appear he would reconsider the job offer to lead a troop to find the missing men. Or whatever might be left of them. But two years out in the worst desert on earth with no supplies? The enlisted men had been right. Major William Conrad and Company F couldn't still be alive. It was a hopeless mission. Besides, he had to get up to Wyoming. There was another job waiting for him there.

"Why don't you send more soldiers?" Fargo asked. "What do you need me for?"

Colonel Power looked Fargo over.

"Because you're the best," he said simply. "Because the officers I've got here are greenhorns. No experience with hard campaigning in the desert. General Coop gave the order—do what you can to rescue Major Conrad. Hiring the Trailsman is the best I can do."

"Sorry, Colonel," Fargo said. "I've got to get to Wyoming. This is a job for the army."

Fargo turned about and let himself out of the office. Behind him, he heard Colonel Power swear under his breath and then slam something down on the desk.

As he made his way past a desk in the main

room, a skinny sergeant glanced up at him curiously. Fargo ignored the gaze and left the building. The low-frame barracks clustered together. Beyond them he could see the sharp dry horizon against the sky, already white with morning heat.

Colonel Power was a determined man, Fargo thought as he strode across the dusty parade ground. He'd seen the kind before. Power was determined to fulfill his duty and to try to get Fargo to lead the expedition. The mission was hopeless, Fargo knew. The vast tract south of Death Valley was man-killing land. Even without the band of renegade Indians who had taken refuge among the dry bluffs.

Fargo felt a twitch between his shoulder blades and he glanced behind him. Through the window of the headquarters building, he saw the dark blue form of Colonel Power watching him. Fargo turned and continued across the yard.

Just then, a bugle sounded and men came pouring out of the barracks which lined the yard. Fargo stepped aside and took a place beside a low wood frame building.

The men mustered for roll call, lining up in rows of eight. Each wore a navy blue wool sack coat with a single row of smart brass buttons and a forage cap. Fargo's sharp eyes swept over the men, spotting the expressionless hard faces of the regular troops, the expectant bright eyes of the callow cadets and recent recruits, and the deep-lined faces of the handful of old soldiers with rows of faded chevrons on their sleeves from the Mexican war.

A tall first lieutenant, his uniform spic and span,

strode forward and snapped his heels together. His bright blond hair, neatly combed, shone in the sun. He was followed by a loping old sergeant.

"Sound off!" the sarge called out. The bugler played again.

"Attention!"

The men snapped into sharp rows, chests out, eyes forward. They were sweating in their dark wool jackets as the morning sun beat down.

Fargo watched for the next half hour as the first lieutenant put the companies through their paces, formed up the guard, announced assigned detail, issued the new passwords, and ordered them through the manual of arms. The lieutenant drove them hard, inspecting the men and assigning one double guard duty for not wearing army-issue socks. At last, the morning drill was over and the men were dismissed. Some moved off in groups while others lingered.

Fargo glanced again toward headquarters. The front door opened and Colonel Power emerged. Several passing officers paused to salute. It was time to get away, Fargo realized. Colonel Power was determined to get what he wanted. And what the colonel wanted was to send Fargo halfway to hell to find a man who might have been dead for two years.

Fargo slipped behind the barrack and headed toward the stable. Just as he turned the corner, Fargo was brought up short. Several soldiers were bringing supplies out of a door and loading them into a wagon. A middle-aged private with a pot belly grunted as he let a heavy burlap sack of grain slide off his shoulders onto the bed of the truck.

The private turned back and scowled as a small slender boy emerged from the doorway, bent almost double under a wooden barrel on his back. The boy stumbled and the barrel pitched sideways, splitting open and spilling waterfalls of yellow cornmeal into the dirt. The boy fell, tumbled into the dust, and rolled to Fargo's feet. The kid looked up, his eyes wide.

Fargo started. The kid's face was grimy and a few wisps of red hair stuck out from beneath his dirty cap. His knickers and jacket fit loosely around his small body. But there was no mistaking what he saw. It was a woman.

Fargo reached down and started to offer his hand, then thought better of it. He smiled down at her for an instant and she started to smile in return, then ducked her head, looking away from him. What the hell was she doing here, Fargo wondered. Probably lovelorn and following some soldier to his outpost. Or else trying to get away from one. Whoever she was, she had her own reasons for disguising herself as a boy.

"Your secret's safe with me," Fargo muttered under his breath.

She shot him a surprised look as she got to her feet, beating the dust out of her clothes and pulling her cap low over her eyes.

"What's going on here?"

Fargo looked up to see the blond first lieutenant standing there, his face red.

"Who's responsible for this?" the officer

snapped, pointing to the busted barrel. "These are United States Army supplies! Who's responsible?"

"That mangy kid!" the private said.

"Seize him," the first lieutenant said. "This is a waste of supplies. It's against regulations."

The private grabbed her by the shoulder, shook her hard, and then dragged her toward the wagon. The lieutenant pulled a horsewhip from the holster beside the driver's seat while the private threw her down into the street. The lieutenant stood above her, coiling the whip around his hand.

"My boy, we're going to learn about military discipline," he snarled.

"Lay off the kid," Fargo said.

The two of them looked up, startled.

"What's it to you, stranger?" the private cut in. "This here boy came in looking for work yesterday. And he's been nothing but a lazy, shirking son of a bitch ever since. He needs to learn what the army's all about."

"I said lay off."

The lieutenant raised the whip above him and suddenly brought it down on her. She cowered and yelped as it snapped across her back, shredding the cloth. The lieutenant barked a cruel laugh and raised the whip again. A crowd of soldiers had gathered around and several were egging on the lieutenant.

Fargo tensed his legs beneath him and sprang toward the two men. He smashed into the lieutenant broadside and kicked out at the private, bringing him down as well. The three of them hit the ground hard. Fargo rolled on top of the lieutenant and kneed him hard in the gut. The air left him and Fargo followed up with a swift uppercut to the jaw that snapped his head backward.

The private rolled and came to his feet. Fargo turned and saw a boot coming straight at his face. He ducked and the kick glanced off the side of his head, exploding pain alongside his ear. Fargo leapt to his feet as the private staggered backward. His powerful arms delivered a shattering right to the man's jaw and then a swift left. The private dropped to his knees and sank to the ground.

"Halt! Halt!"

Fargo heard the unmistakable click of a rifle. He shook his head to clear it and looked up. A crowd of men encircled them. A soldier stood a few feet away, the long barrel of a Winchester aimed right at his heart. Behind the soldier stood Colonel Power.

"What the hell is going on here?" Power asked.

"This man jumped us," the lieutenant sputtered as he got to his feet. The private sat up, rubbing his jaw, his eyes flashing rage at Fargo. "I was just disciplining that boy over there."

She was still cowering near the wagon, hiding her face beneath the shallow brim of her cap. She was obviously uncomfortable being the center of attention. Fargo wondered again what she was doing in this godforsaken fort.

"These two were ganging up on the boy," Fargo said.

Colonel Power looked Fargo up and down. The soldiers standing around them listened closely.

"I could charge you with assaulting an officer,"

Power said thoughtfully. "Assaulting *two* officers. Could put you in the guardhouse until I get a tribunal together. That could take a long time."

"I'm a civilian," Fargo said hotly.

"I'm in charge here," the colonel said. "And you're a troublemaker."

Fargo stood considering his options. He sure as hell couldn't shoot his way out of the fort. And even if he managed to slip away, the colonel would press charges and he'd be a wanted man. Damn it. The colonel could make an issue out of an assault charge. And, out of sheer cussedness, he could keep him locked up as long as he wanted.

"Unless you go to Fort Chingo," the colonel added quietly.

At the colonel's words, the girl started and got to her feet, looking from one to the other of them. The colonel took no notice of her.

"Cash up front," Fargo said. Accepting the job, he realized, was the only way out. "Gold, not greenbacks."

"*After* you return with the major," the colonel said.

"No deal."

"Three months in the clink. To start. Take him."

Two soldiers stepped toward him. Fargo held up his hand and they halted.

"Then I want my pay held in a locked box for my return."

"You don't trust me?" The colonel's brows shot up and the men standing around him shifted uneasily.

"No, I don't."

Colonel Power whirled about and started to leave. Then, as if in an afterthought, he turned back.

"All right. You leave at dawn. Your men will be mustered on the parage ground at 0500 hours, along with supplies." He turned to go.

There was a flurry of motion beside the wagon and the disguised woman hurled herself at Fargo's feet and clutched him around the knees.

"Take me with you," she said, looking up at Fargo. In her eyes was a kind of rare desperation.

The colonel turned back.

"What's this?"

"Sorry," Fargo said to her. He leaned down and disengaged her. "That's tough country out there. Not fit for a . . . a boy."

"Who *is* this kid?" the colonel snapped.

"Came in yesterday," the private said. He stepped toward the woman and seized her arm. "Been a passel of trouble ever since."

She tried to shake him off. The private drew back his arm. He aimed a blow at her but struck the cap, which flew off her head. She grabbed for the cap, but missed it and then she glared defiantly. Her auburn hair glistened in the sun, two thick braids wound over her head.

"What the hell?" the private muttered.

"What's a woman doing here?" the lieutenant sputtered. "This is against regulations! Who's responsible?"

Colonel Power took a step forward and looked down at her. She stepped up to him, chin in the air. Fargo couldn't help but admire her spirit.

21

"You again? You goddamn idiot!" Powers said to her. "You're going to get yourself killed, you know. Go along if you want to. Just get out of my fort! I've had enough."

The colonel left hastily and the crowd of men around them slowly melted away. The lieutenant marched off stiffly and the private skulked toward the barracks, still glowering at Fargo and the woman.

"Thank you for what you did," she said, looking up at Fargo. Her face was streaked with grime and sweat, her hair tangled. But her pale blue eyes were forthright and ringed with long red lashes which glistened in the sun.

"Who are you?" Fargo asked.

"Come on," she said. They walked together to a nearby pump where she washed up, ignoring Fargo. She removed her jacket to reveal a man's shirt that clung to her slender waist. She rolled up the sleeves and pumped water into the stone trough, leaning over to splash it on her face and neck. The shirt fell open and Fargo glimpsed the curve of one small round breast and dark nipple. She straightened up, dashing the water from her eyes. Her honey skin was smooth and lovely, her lips and cheeks pink. She quickly loosened her hair and combed it out with her fingers, letting the reddish locks fall around her shoulders. Then she expertly pinned it up again.

"There, that's better," she said at last. She dried her hand on her trousers and offered it to him with a big smile.

"What's this all about?" Fargo asked, pointing at her boy's clothing.

"I like adventure," she said defiantly.

Fargo looked at her.

"My name's Katie," she admitted at last, dropping the heroic pretense. "Katie Conrad."

Fargo shook her small hand, impressed by her self-possession.

"Conrad. Major Conrad's . . ."

"Daughter."

Fargo studied her for a moment. Yes, the determined jaw and the high intelligent brow were the same features he's noticed in the photograph of Major Conrad. But her eyes were blue, clear, and trusting.

"So, you want to come along to Fort Chingo and rescue him?"

"Exactly."

"No," Fargo said, reluctantly releasing her hand. "Between this fort and that one is the worst territory outside of Hades. I admire your gumption, getting dressed up like a boy and sneaking into this fort. But I'm leading that expedition tomorrow. And it's not fit country for a woman."

"A nice speech, mister," Katie said, one hand on her hip, her eyes narrowing. "But let me just tell you that I'm not taking no for an answer. My father's been out there alone for two years and the U.S. Army hasn't done a damned thing about it. I wrote letters, and I went to Washington, D.C. I even came out here last year and agitated. That's why the colonel and I don't get along so well."

"You must have put the squeeze on General Coop, too."

"I did! Wrote him a hundred letters."

"And let me guess," Fargo went on with a smile. "You finally hustled some newspaper journalist to take up your cause."

She nodded.

"That's what finally got the general's attention," Katie said with a note of triumph. "And if you don't let me go with you tomorrow, I swear I'll follow you every step of the way. On foot if I have to."

Fargo looked down at her, considering. She was damned tough for a young woman. And beautiful, too. His eyes traveled down the long line of her throat to the unbuttoned neckline of her shirt. But the trip wasn't going to be a Sunday picnic by any means.

"Leave it to me," he said at last. "You can't help out there. If your father's alive, I'll bring him back."

"No," Katie said desperately, her face reddening. "You don't understand. I've *got* to go. I have these dreams. I hear him calling me. It's fiery hot and I find him all alone and sick . . ."

Fargo waited, looking down at her. Tears filled her pale blue eyes. She blinked them back.

"What if he's already dead?" Fargo asked quietly.

"No!" Katie said. "No, I can *feel* that he's still alive. I know it sounds crazy, but I *know* he's out there."

Fargo stood looking at her. She was the kind of

woman who would stop at nothing. And she really believed this dream. It was what had driven her to take on the entire U.S. Army, including General Coop. And he didn't doubt for a moment that she'd follow him on foot if he started off.

"Tomorrow at dawn," he said, nodding slowly.

"Thank you!" Katie said, suddenly hugging him, her soft body pressing against his hard, lean muscles. Then she stepped away quickly, her eyes serious. "Thank you for everything. I don't even know your name."

"Fargo. Skye Fargo."

She searched his eyes with deep interest.

"They call you the Trailsman."

"That's right."

"I've heard your reputation. Folks say you can outride, outshoot, outtrack any man in the West. Now I *know* we're going to make it."

They smiled at one another. From a distance, he heard the march of troops as the guard changed. Morning was passing.

"I'd better get my things ready," she said, turning away.

"One knapsack," he warned.

"I'm not bringing my silk dresses!" she said laughingly over her shoulder.

"See you at dawn," he called after her.

In the predawn shadows of the parade ground, a dozen men stood in a scraggly line alongside a mountain wagon. Fargo jerked open the flap of canvas and looked inside. There were kegs of coffee beans and salt port alongside boxes of hardtack.

The usual grim army-issue fare. There would be just enough to get them through the trip, he saw. He turned away and inspected the huge water barrels hanging down beside the wagon. They were sufficient, but barely.

The wagon was hitched to six mules, stringy animals, but they'd make it. The wagon itself had seen better days, too, although a glance underneath told him it was solid enough. He straightened up at the sound of approaching footsteps.

Colonel Power approached, followed by the blond first lieutenant carrying a knapsack.

"Is everything in order?" the colonel asked.

"I don't know yet," Fargo said. He turned away from the wagon and walked down the line of men. He felt their eyes on him as he slowly paraded in front of them. It was a mangy bunch for the most part, a different breed from the smart soldiers he had seen the day before. Their faces were suspicious. They wore pieces of mismatched uniforms. Each man had a rucksack on his back and carried his rifle beside him.

"Atten-hut!" the lieutenant called out.

The men pulled themselves into attention. Fargo continued down the line and stopped in front of a fresh-faced kid with freckles across his nose, standing with his chest out.

"How old are you, son?" Fargo asked him.

"Eight . . . eighteen! Sir!" the kid stuttered.

"Like hell," Fargo muttered and continued up the line. At the end, he stopped in front of a sergeant. The man was an old campaigner, his grizzled cheeks silver-flecked and his eyes tough and hard. A row of chevrons were sewn on his shirt.

"How many enlistments you seen, soldier?" Fargo asked.

"Seven," the man said. His eyes flickered toward Fargo's face, then away.

"Name?"

"Joe Dade. Sergeant. Thirteenth Infantry. Company B."

Fargo turned away. The only one of the bunch who looked useful was this sergeant.

"That's the best you can round up for me?" Fargo asked Colonel Power.

"All fine men," he boomed. "Now, get going."

"Horses. Mules," Fargo said. "Where are they?"

"Infantry," Power replied. "They'll march it. Over the long haul, a good infantry can go just as fast as the cavalry. You'll see."

"I don't care how fast they can march," Fargo snapped. "I want eleven mules for these men. And a remuda, a second string. And add two more mules to the wagon. Good ones. And a horse for Miss Conrad. A fast one." If they got into bad trouble, Fargo thought, he wanted Katie to have the opportunity for escape.

Power opened his mouth to protest, then thought better of it and relayed the order. In a few minutes, additional mules were brought up from the stables. A soldier arrived with a broken-down hay-burner with a bad sway back.

"I said a *fast* horse," Fargo snapped. The soldier shot a look at the colonel and returned to the stable. He was back a few minutes later with a smart-looking chestnut. Fargo laid his hand on the horse's flank. The mare started and lifted her hooves. The horse would be fast all right. And spirited.

Fargo spotted Katie Conrad heading toward them. She wore a riding skirt, boots, and a leather vest. A wide-brimmed hat hung down her back and in one hand she carried a small leather bag.

"That's *it*?" he asked, looking down at the small bag.

"I travel light," she said, handing it to him.

"How's your riding?" he said with a grin, stowing it in the wagon.

"This mine?" she asked, nodding at the chestnut.

He nodded and Katie patted its nose and immediately swung up onto the horse. The chestnut gave a start and started to rear. Kate expertly pulled its head down low and patted its neck with long strokes. The horse moved nervously, stomping and skittering, then quieted. Fargo felt relieved. Katie kept her head on a horse. He hoped that was a sign of how she'd be on the trail.

"Time to march," Colonel Power said. "It's getting late."

Fargo realized the officer was damned eager for them to leave and he wondered why for a fleeting moment. He turned and whistled and the black-and-white Ovaro, which had been standing beside the fence, untethered, cantered toward him. The faithful pinto nickered and playfully nosed his shirt. Fargo mounted. A third horse was being led toward the parade yard and the lieutenant prepared to mount.

"First Lieutenant Martin Pike will be coming

with you as the commanding officer," Colonel Power said.

"Fine," Fargo snapped. "But I'm in charge of this expedition. What I say, goes."

"Yes, yes, of course," Power put in hastily.

"Just a moment," Fargo said, looking down at the colonel. The Ovaro shifted beneath him. "Let's get it straight. Here and now. *I'm* in charge."

"Absolutely," the colonel said agreeably.

"You hear that, Lieutenant?" Fargo asked. Lieutenant Pike was sitting straight up on his horse, listening.

"Is that an order, sir?" the lieutenant asked the colonel.

"This is an *order*, Lieutenant," Colonel Power said, impatience edging his voice. "A *direct* order. Skye Fargo is in charge of this expedition."

The lieutenant saluted smartly, but did not meet Fargo's gaze. Fargo shrugged.

"Let's go," Fargo said.

Sergeant Dade had lined up the men beside their mules. On his order they mounted. Fargo took the lead, riding beside Katie. Half the men rode just behind them, followed by the two wagons, the lieutenant, and the remainder of the men.

They passed through the wide open wooden gates of Fort Desoto. To the east, needles of brilliant light from the rising sun pierced the scattered cloud wisps in the wide, clear sky. From northeast to southwest, the Old Spanish Trail snaked its way across the low greasewood hills.

Fargo turned about in his saddle and looked back at the line of men and mules which followed him.

The wooden fort, alone on the wide barren flat, grew smaller in the distance. There was a hard pull ahead, he thought, one of the hardest he'd ever faced.

Fargo, with Katie Conrad riding beside him, turned the Ovaro northward, seeking and then finding the trail that led north and west to Broken Oak's Trading Post and finally to Fort Chingo.

It was only later that Skye Fargo realized he should have suspected something. Should have guessed the colonel was holding out on him in more ways than one. But on that bright morning, his thoughts were on the men and the woman he was leading into danger. So, he only noticed it in passing and didn't stop to ask himself why. As they turned northward, Fargo's keen eyes read that the trail to Broken Oak's Trading Post looked as if no one had traveled on it for a long, long time.

2

Fargo paused, mopped his brow, and turned about in the saddle to look down on the ragged line which followed him. The two wagons—one with oats for the horses and mules, the other with the supplies for the men—creaked and groaned up the rocky trail. The men on mules hunched in the saddles, their hat brims low and navy blue uniforms sweat-soaked in the blazing sun. Katie Conrad slouched on her mount, which walked steadily among the mules, its chestnut hide glistening with sweat. Only Lieutenant Pike seemed unaffected by the scorching waves of heat. He rode erect, the buttons of his uniform sparkled gold in the unrelenting brightness.

Above, the cloudless sky was bleached white. All around them, the humpbacked Soda Mountains baked in the shadowless light. The brown and gray and yellow of the greasewood and grasses were faded, almost colorless. The occasional patches of white alkali reflected painfully. Nothing moved but the slow, oily waves of heat rising from the barren land around them. Nevertheless, Fargo scanned the hills.

It was always just when you thought there was nothing out there that something always appeared. Usually something dangerous. Fargo's keen eyes swept the sere hillsides, seeking any sign of movement. But the hills remained empty, undulating in the heat.

Fargo tried to imagine being Major Conrad, sent out into this godforsaken country to establish an outpost. Five years without seeing a green tree or a body of water. Five years in the parching desert sun. A man had to have a certain iron character to survive out here for long. But five years . . .

Fargo pulled out his canteen and took a swig of the warmed water. There was no need to stop. If there was a spot of shade around, he would call a halt and let the men rest for a few hours until the sun lowered. But there wasn't a shadow bigger than a man's hand. He let the Ovaro pick its way down the rocky trail.

By the end of the day, when the red ball of sun touched the tops of the Granite Mountains, they were descending the slopes of the Soda Mountains. Fargo spotted a shallow gully at the foot of a hill and headed toward it. It was just right for their first night's camp. In the rock-strewn cleft, he saw a swath of sand and a touch of green among the yellow grasses. Might be water. He brought the Ovaro to a halt.

Fargo dismounted as the soldiers pulled up around him and came to a stop. They had done well for the first day, making twenty-five miles with only two brief stops for water. Four more days like this one and they'd be at Fort Chingo. But, Fargo knew, each day the soldiers and mules would be more exhausted, the heat and sun taking its toll on man and animal alike. Each day would drag on more slowly, each mile of baked dust would seem longer and longer.

"Dismount!" Lieutenant Pike shouted, bringing his horse forward and sliding down. "Make camp!"

The soldiers hobbled the mules. The wagons pulled into an L formation and the mules were led out of the traces. Katie slid down from the chestnut and stumbled, then caught herself against the saddle.

"A long day's ride," Fargo said, catching up the reins of her horse.

"I'll be all right," Katie said, rubbing her backside and smiling ruefully.

Fargo tethered their two horses nearby among some dry grasses. As he walked back toward Katie, he saw three soldiers pitching a canvas tent at the bottom of the draw. He hastened toward them.

"What are you doing?" he interrupted. One of the three, the freckled-faced kid, looked up.

"This is for the . . . the lady," he answered, looking beyond Fargo to where Katie stood. A deep blush started from beneath the kid's collar and rose slowly beneath his freckles.

"What's your name, son?" Fargo asked.

"Tommy Gibbons! Sir!"

The two other men glanced up at Fargo tiredly, their faces dust-caked and drawn.

"Well, Tommy," Fargo said, "is this your first campaign?"

"Yes, sir!"

"Then tell me why this arroyo is here in the middle of this desert?"

The boy looked about him at the steep walls of the gully, confusion on his face.

"Dunno, sir."

The two other men shifted impatiently.

"Come along, kid," one of them muttered.

Fargo shot them a dark look and they shut up.

"Water," Fargo said. "Rainwater. Flash floods. Ever heard of 'em?"

The kid looked about him quizzically.

"Don't look like it ever rains here."

"But when it does," Fargo said, "there's nothing to hold the water back. And it happens fast. The water races through these gullies and sweeps everything away. Including young ladies in tents. Now, you want that to happen?"

The kid shook his head quickly, the blush deepening.

"Pitch the tent up there," Fargo instructed, indicating a low rise.

"Can't do that," one of the other men said. "We got orders. Lieutenant Pike. He said pitch it down here."

Fargo wheeled about and strode toward the supply wagons where several of the men were unloading feed. The rest of the men stood about idly watching. The lieutenant leaned on the wagon wheel, swigging water from his canteen.

"Put that bag over there," the lieutenant barked. "No, move it over another foot." The two men carrying the heavy bag of oats exchanged a secret, exasperated look.

"Pike!" Fargo said.

The lieutenant turned, his face tight.

"Are you the fool who ordered those men to pitch Miss Conrad's tent down in that gully? You ever heard of flash floods?"

"Easier to protect her in a gully," the lieutenant spat. "Defensive strategy. Of course, a *civilian* wouldn't know about such things. Leave the military affairs to me, *Mr.* Fargo."

Fargo stepped up to him. First Lieutenant Martin Pike wasn't a short man, but Fargo bested him by a good four inches. The lieutenant drew himself up to his full height and squared his shoulders. He looked up at Fargo defiantly.

"I'm in charge of this expedition," Fargo said in a low voice. "Colonel's orders. And it's a good thing. Because obviously, you don't know what the hell you're doing."

The lieutenant's nostrils flared and his lips tightened. One of the men standing nearby chuckled softly. The lieutenant whirled about at the sound.

"Who was that?" Pike snapped, looking toward the soldiers. A line of blank-faced men met his gaze. The lieutenant spun about on his heels and stalked away.

"All right," Fargo called out. "Move that tent up on this rise." The three soldiers jumped to obey him. "And, you! Hobble the mules closer to the wagons. Get 'em watered and fed. Now! You! Get a campfire built and you two fetch more fuel. You three over there, get spades and follow me. An hour's work and you can rest for the night!"

The soldiers moved into action, but except for

the young recruits, they weren't quick about it. Fargo led three men down to the bottom of the draw, where he had seen the hint of green. He instructed them to dig and they started. In an hour, as twilight was falling, they had made a big watery mudhole.

"Get the mules down here to take a drink," Fargo told them. "It will save us water."

Fargo headed toward the blazing campfire, which was redolent of mesquite, and sat down on a rock beside it. A fat soldier had taken charge of the cooking and had pulled crates and kegs out of the supply wagon. The desert air was cold. Katie emerged from the tent, freshened up with her loosed hair hanging down around her shoulders. She spotted Fargo and joined him. The cook, his shirtsleeves rolled to his elbows, slung the hash from the kettle.

"It ain't good, but it's the best I can do with army beans," the cook apologized as he handed tin plates to Katie and Fargo.

"I'm sure it's fine," Katie said kindly. She dug in her fork and tried a bite, chewing slowly, a look of disgust spreading slowly across her face. Her eyes darted about, looking for a way to spit out the beans.

"Swallow it," Fargo said quietly. "You'll need the strength." He took a mouthful and chewed. Hell, it was bad. Real bad. The beans had been highly seasoned, but he could taste the mustiness of mold. And his teeth came together with a crunch on a small stone, which he spat out. He swallowed the beans. "Awful," he concluded.

"Welcome to the army," a voice said with a sarcastic laugh.

Just behind them sat the grizzled Sergeant Dade, his plate in one hand and a forkful of beans in the other. The cook heaped beans on the plates for the other men. They all ate in silence. Lieutenant Pike had taken his plate sulkily and retreated to the other side of the wagons. The men ate quickly, then busied themselves about the camp. Dade sat whittling.

Katie ate a few more bites, then put down the plate and rested her head on her hands, staring into the fire. Fargo finished his beans and watched the golden flickering light play on her long pale lashes. Her eyes were deep with thought, about her father, no doubt.

"What was he like?" Fargo asked, watching her.

"Wonderful," she said, turning her brimming eyes toward him. "He was brave and strong. Devoted to my . . . my mother." Her voice grew thick with emotion. Fargo waited, his eyes searching her pretty face as she swallowed hard.

"My mother died out in Kansas," Katie continued. "She had gone to see my father and she caught smallpox." There was a long silence as she gazed beyond the fire, as if witnessing the painful past. "Father never came back East after that. He wrote to me, but I never saw him again. He asked to be transferred out here and then . . ."

"Then he volunteered to get out there and establish Fort Chingo," Fargo said thoughtfully. It all made sense. The major, grief-stricken by his wife's death, volunteering for hardship duty. Sometimes

a man had to get death out of his system and sometimes going to hell and back was the best way to
do it. Still, there was the question of why Major
Conrad had disobeyed Colonel Power's orders to
return to Fort Desoto. That didn't make sense.
Conrad might have been grieving, but if he had a
daughter in the East, he shouldn't have been sui-
cidal. Fargo shook his head and then caught Sergeant Dade's eye.

The old sarge sat looking at Katie Conrad, a wry
smile on his face. It wasn't as if the soldier was
amused, far from it. Rather, it was an expression
of profound irony. Dade suddenly caught Fargo
looking at him and he started. The sarge's face was
an immediate illegible blank as he got to his feet
and moved away. Fargo knew the sergeant had his
own opinions about Major Conrad. He'd take him
aside later and ask what he knew.

Kate's eyelids were drooping and soon closed. In
another moment, she sagged against him, asleep.

Fargo cradled Katie against him, feeling her soft
warmth moving gently with each breath. She
shifted and her face fell forward, buried between
his thighs. She moaned in her sleep. Fargo felt the
pressure of her face against him and her hot breath
between his legs. He felt himself grow hard as he
looked down on the curves of her slender back and
hips and legs. But he didn't move. The fat cook
raised his eyebrows, gave Fargo a grin, and very
gingerly passed over a hot cup of coffee. Several
of the soldiers walking by the fire shot him envious
looks. Fargo sat sipping the coffee, enjoying the
weight of Katie's head against him.

The cook gathered up the tin plates and the clatter awoke Katie. Her eyes flew open and she sat up with a start.

"Oh!" she exclaimed, shrinking away from him. She hastily got to her feet and walked hurriedly away toward the tent, obviously embarrassed. Several of the soldiers guffawed at her obvious embarrassment.

"Good night!" Fargo called after her. She didn't answer.

Fargo sat looking into the embers of the campfire as he wondered about Major Conrad. The desert night was eerily still. Once Fargo heard a wild flapping of wings, probably an owl hunting a desert rat. Another time he heard a yip of a kit fox from nearby.

His thoughts went back to Fort Desoto and Colonel Power. He felt a wave of anger at the way he'd been roped into this mission. Damn the colonel. It was hopeless, anyway, he knew. Major Conrad and Company F were sure to be dead after two years and no word from them. And Katie was the kind of determined woman who wouldn't believe it until she saw it with her own eyes.

And what would they find at the end of Rio Chingo? Fargo had seen it countless times before. An abandoned outpost, a flagpole with a tattered flag, a couple of low adobe walls pitted by bullets, skeletons with tattered uniforms. The horses, weapons, buttons, and boots would have been carried off by marauding Indians. An outpost of ghosts.

It was hopeless. And if it hadn't been for Colonel

Power, he'd be on his way to Cheyenne. He shook his head.

"Yep. The colonel's a real bastard," the sarge said quietly, as if reading Fargo's thoughts. He got to his feet and stretched, then made his way toward where the other soldiers slept.

Fargo took a turn once around the camp and was about to turn in when he saw the tent flap being pulled back. Katie emerged in a long white cotton gown, a shawl around her shoulders and carrying a tin mug. She smiled when she saw him, her face lit by the dying fire.

"I was just going for some water."

"I'll get it," Fargo offered. He returned in a moment with the mug filled and stood watching her as she drank. Her auburn hair was loose about her shoulders. She glanced up at him and cleared her throat, looking nervously around.

"Where are you sleeping?"

Fargo raised his brows at the question.

"I'll pull my bedroll out over there somewhere."

Katie smiled slowly up at him.

"There's plenty of room in my tent for two," she said very softly. "I like adventure."

Fargo stepped forward and started to take her in his arms. She glanced about again, but all the men were bedded down. She put a hand against his chest.

"Only, you have to creep out before dawn," she whispered. "I've got my reputation to protect. Promise?"

Fargo followed her into the tent.

She stretched out on the blankets, suddenly shy.

Fargo lay down beside her, then leaned over to kiss her lightly. Her lips were like honey, with a sun-warmed sweet taste. Her hands came up behind his head to stroke his neck tentatively.

Fargo slowly explored her mouth with his tongue, penetrating deeper with slow strokes. She moaned and he felt her body go limp. He stroked the slender length of her side through her nightgown, stroking up toward her breast, enjoying the softness of it in the palm of his hand. She fumbled with the buttons and then he slipped his hand inside, very softly circling her delicate nipple. She shuddered.

"At the fort ... how did you ... know I ... was a woman?" she asked, the words coming out between her panting. Fargo thought of her dressed as a boy.

"Ankles. Neck."

He unbuttoned her nightgown slowly.

"Wrists. Cheekbones."

He kissed her neck downward, heading toward her breasts and pulling back the nightgown.

"Other things. None of it looked like a boy to me."

He felt her smile into the darkness as he kissed one breast and then the other, flicking his tongue over her tender nipples as she breathed into the darkness. Fargo felt himself straining against his jeans, heavy and hard. He stripped off his shirt and unbuckled his belt. He felt her hands exploring him through his jeans. She gasped in the darkness, feeling the length of him, confined. He stripped and lay down beside her and he felt her light touch again on him, exploring down his belly and then softly stroking the long length of him. He pulled up her nightgown slowly, and she pulled it off over her head as he nuzzled her, inhaling her musky sweetness.

"Please. Now," Katie murmured.

He pulled himself on top of her and felt her legs go around him, her ankles hooked behind his back as the hard tip of him sought her softness. He slipped inside of her, gently, teasingly, feeling as if he belonged there. Her soft wetness seemed comfortingly familiar and he stroked slowly, without urgency, as he felt her petals enlarge. She met his every thrust, taking him deeper and deeper into her. He stroked her hard button and she gasped. He felt her contracting and the spurting release began in him, slowly and exquisitely, building with slow inevitability and finally releasing, squirting deep into her with powerful jabs. Fargo stroked in and out until he was completely dry, then fell onto the blankets beside her, exhausted, complete. He pulled her close to him in the dark.

"We do that well together," she murmured.

Fargo stroked her hair in answer as he felt sleep well up around him.

Trouble started the next morning. Fargo left Katie's tent well before dawn. He'd fed the Ovaro, then set off to scout the area. A startled coyote ran from a nearby bush and a few kangaroo rats bounded into their burrows. The sun rose white and hot in the cloudless sky as the dew sparkled on the bare twigs and sparse grass. Fargo started walking in a wide spiral around the campsite, angling outward, his sharp eyes searching the ground, reading the landscape the way some men read books. He spotted the tracks of rodents, foxes, and coyotes. And then on his first pass around, just to the southwest, about a hundred yards out and well secreted beneath a clump of sage, he saw the body.

Fargo turned the corpse face up and recognized one of the old regulars, a skinny one with a beard. His throat slit from ear to ear, the blood soaking his uniform and the ground beneath him. His eyes were open and staring at the sky as if in disbelief, jaw slack, one hand clutched the butt of his pistol.

Fargo glanced about and found bootprints in the bare dust. Also a stinking damp area of dirt. The soldier had wandered out beyond the guard circle to relieve himself and there, in the dark, somebody had jumped him from behind. Fargo bent down and looked closely at the prints, watching the grains of dust stir in the early morning breeze. Another hour and the tracks would be nearly obliterated. The solitary stranger's tracks led toward camp and then became a short trail of crushed grasses where the man had crawled forward. Fargo followed the trail to a spot behind a short fringe of rabbitbrush. He knelt and looked toward the camp. From here, the unknown watcher had had a perfect view of everything in camp—how many men, how many horses, how many guns.

Fargo swore silently to himself as he retraced the prints past the body and followed them away across the grass-tufted plain. A quarter mile away, the bootprints merged with hoofprints that led westward. Whoever had spied on them during the night had gotten a good look and then made off again. And the army men watching hadn't had a clue he was there. All but one. And he was dead.

Double guards every night from now on, Fargo decided. And periphery guards, too, circling farther out from the camp, the way the Indians did. And passwords, fifteen-minute checks. Damn, the soldiers had been lax. One had been murdered and the others hadn't even missed him!

Fargo wondered about the mysterious visitor. The bootprints and the fact that the horse was shod indicated it was not an Indian. A Mexican *bandito*, maybe? Or maybe an Indian with stolen boots and horse. Fargo's brow was thick with thought as he reentered the camp.

Even before he arrived, Fargo heard the stentorian tones of the lieutenant barking orders. He found most of the soldiers slouching about while Pike concentrated all his attention on directing the three men taking down Katie's tent.

"No, no, no!" Lieutenant Pike screamed. "Take the poles out *first*, then pull up the stakes! That's regulations! Poles first, then stakes!" The lieutenant ordered them to put the stakes back in the ground and do it properly. Meanwhile, the other men watched. Katie Conrad hovered in the background, looking on.

"What's going on here?" Fargo demanded.

The lieutenant spun about, his face reddening at the sound of Fargo's voice

"These men don't know the first thing about military discipline," the lieutenant sputtered. "As soon as this tent is properly stowed, we're having morning roll call and inspection."

"Hold on!" Fargo said, his voice tight with fury. "There's no parade in the field."

"Regulations! It's regulations!" the lieutenant protested. He drew a small military manual from his breast pocket and began flipping through it. "Morning roll call ..." he muttered, trying to find the page.

"He doesn't know there's no morning muster," the old sarge said under his breath, loud enough for Fargo to hear. "He's never been out of the fort."

"That's enough!" Fargo snapped at Pike.

Pike continued rifling the pages of his rule book and the other men moved off sullenly, ignoring Fargo.

"Where's Johnny Blue?" one soldier muttered, looking about.

"He got his throat slit," Fargo said, jerking his thumb in the direction of the corpse. "He's lying out there."

Fargo had their attention now. The men fell silent and stared at him. Katie gasped.

"Wow," Tommy Gibbons muttered, almost to himself.

"Last night we had a visitor. Lone man. Got within a hundred feet of this camp." Fargo paused and looked about at the men as his words sank in.

"That's ... that's ridiculous!" Pike sputtered. "My men were on guard ..."

"Your men were walking around blind as bats," Fargo retorted. The lieutenant stalked off to go view the body as if he didn't believe what Fargo had told him. Fargo turned to address the rest of the men.

"Tonight, we're going to have guard drill for an hour before we turn in. And double guards from now on. And meanwhile, whoever was watching us knows who we are and what we've got with us. Water, horses, and guns don't come easy out here." Fargo paused as he silently added "and a woman." Katie Conrad, if she'd been spotted, would just be one more reason for an ambush.

"Now, let's get Johnny Blue buried and get on the trail," Fargo snapped. "Ride doubled up, guns at the ready! You men get the mules watered again and into the traces," Fargo said. "Now!"

"You ain't our commanding officer," one said. Fargo shot a look at him. He'd noticed the man before, a thick-browed man with his eyes set too close together.

"What's your name, soldier?" Fargo demanded.

"Sullivan. Bill Sullivan," the man said defiantly. "What's it to you?"

"I'm in charge of this operation," Fargo said, his eyes narrow. "Don't give me trouble or I'll make you damn sorry."

Sullivan shrugged lazily. One of the others pulled on his arm and three of them moved away toward the mules. He'd have trouble with that one, Fargo thought, watching Billy Sullivan go.

Pike returned wordlessly from looking at the soldier's body. The men moved about, the young ones quickly and ineffectually, the older ones shirking as much of the hard labor of packing up as possible. Fargo watched them covertly as he saddled the

Ovaro and the chestnut. Suddenly, Pike's shouts drew him to the other side of the wagons.

"Put that man in irons!" the lieutenant was screaming. One of the other soldiers brought forward iron shackles hesitantly. A carrot-headed private stood looking down at his feet. He glanced up fearfully at Fargo.

"What's going on here?" Fargo demanded.

"This man isn't wearing regulation boots!"

Fargo broke out into a guffaw.

Pike drew himself up in a fury.

"You can laugh," Pike said. "But these men need discipline. First it's nonregulation boots. Then they'll disobey orders! Put those shackles on that man!"

"My feet swelled up," the redheaded boy said. "Had to get something bigger."

Fargo stepped forward and thrust aside the iron manacles.

"I'm . . . I'm the commanding officer here," Pike protested.

"And I'm in charge," Fargo said. "From now on, there is one regulation on this campaign." His lake blue eyes were icy as he looked about at the soldiers, who had dropped their work and gathered around to watch the disagreement. "One. Do what I tell you."

The men shifted uneasily. They were a sorry bunch, Fargo thought again, looking around at them. There were boys like the carrot-topped kid and the one named Tommy Gibbons. And then there were the surly types like Billy Sullivan. There wasn't a good soldier among them except for Sergeant Dade, who stood at the back of the group, shaking his head in disgust.

Fargo led his Ovaro and Katie's chestnut to the mud hole for water. When he arrived, he found it had dried up overnight. That was typical, he thought. There were places in the desert where the water appeared for a few hours or a few days, and then disappeared again, running far beneath the dry surface, out of reach and coming up somewhere else. Fargo fetched water from the barrel and gave the horses their allotment as he gave them a cursory brushing to get the dust out of their coats. Desert heat was hell on horses. Even worse than for mules. The chestnut was a good horse, spirited, young, and strong. But, over the long haul, it would be no match for the sturdiness of his black-and-white pinto. Katie walked toward him, her cheeks pink and eyes bright.

"Sleep well?" he asked innocently, holding the chestnut for her so that she could mount.

"Who do you think it was out there?" Katie said in a serious tone.

Fargo shrugged.

"Nothing to worry about," he lied. "Maybe some lone deserter who wanted to see what we were up to."

"Like hell!" Katie snapped. She whirled about and mounted, then sat looking down at him, her face reddening with fury. Her words tumbled out. "Don't forget who you're talking to, *Mr.* Fargo. I'm the daughter of Major William Conrad. I'm *not* stupid. whoever was out there was a scout. And whoever he was scouting for is likely to attack."

Fargo held up his hands.

"Easy, easy," he said. "Sorry I underestimated you. But if I'd known you were so pretty when you're angry, I'd have done it on purpose."

Katie swallowed once, then slowly smiled.

"Okay," she said, a chuckle in her voice. She blinked her pale blue eyes once, serious again. "Now, will you answer my question. Who do you think it was?"

Fargo grinned up at her. She was a hellcat for sure and yet soft in all the right places. God, he liked her spirit.

"He wore boots and his horse was shod."

"So," Katie said thoughtfully, "not an Indian."

"Not necessarily," Fargo said. She thought for a moment, and then nodded, her eyes on the horizon.

"I can shoot," Katie said. She pulled aside her vest to reveal a leather belt and holster around her slender waist. A carved silver Dimick derringer glittered in the morning sun.

"Nice pistol," Fargo said, a sly note in his voice. "Do you want to see mine again?"

He paused and enjoyed her slow blush as he grinned up at her. It was a pleasure to tease her, he thought.

'But it's not much good at long range," Fargo said, his tone serious again. "Keep it loaded in case you get stuck at close range. But you ought to have a rifle."

Fargo fetched her a Pennsylvania trade musket that sported brass rivets in the wooden butt. It was a solid, dependable weapon. Easy to load and shoot. Katie took the firearm and held it against her shoulder, looking down the long barrel. She lowered it and smiled down at Fargo.

"Hope you won't need it," he said.

Katie nodded and spurred the chestnut toward the wagons. Fargo stood looking after her. He'd never met another woman like Katie Conrad, with her iron determination and her intriguing mixture of toughness and graceful femininity. He remembered what it had been like being held inside her. He could chew on that all day, he thought. And look forward to more.

As the sun inched up the eastern sky, Fargo led them northwest across a wide alkali flat. A stunted Joshua tree stood on a low hillock, its dying arms reaching upward. Occasional clumps of yellow grass and low sage dotted the plain, but wide stretches of the blinding white and ochre flat were barren. To the north, the Granite Mountains were low and hazy blue against the bright desert floor. They looked cool and inviting, but Fargo knew as they drew closer, the mountains would turn sere and dry like the rest of the landscape. He watched as the liquid silver lakes formed, glittered, and retreated before them in the shimmering light, mirages that would drive a thirsty man mad with frustrated desire.

At noon, Fargo called a halt beside an outcropping of sandstone. The men, tired and sweating, took turns standing in the small sliver of shade to the north side of the sun-baked rocks. Fargo noted that the carrot-topped kid was now wearing the manacles, his wrist bound in front of him. The lieutenant had ignored Fargo's command and handcuffed the kid. Fargo swore under his breath and vowed he'd deal with Pike when they got to the trading post. Fargo cautioned the soldiers not to drink too much water and then climbed to the top of the rocks in the blistering heat. He stood, boots braced in the cracks of the dry stone, and looked out over the flat.

Somewhere at the foot of the Granite Mountains lay Broken Oak's Trading Post. They'd arrive by nightfall. His lake blue eyes swept the empty land and his thoughts turned to the half-breed trader. As he descended the rocks and signaled for the group to remount, Fargo examined his memories of Broken Oak, one by one. Even as he angled the Ovaro to the head of the line and kept his piercing gaze ever on the silent landscape, his thoughts were on the wiry man he had met so long ago.

It had been in Kansas when Fargo had first come upon Broken Oak, the energetic, sharp-faced, quick-talking trader who plied his wares from a wagon, crisscrossing the high plains. He'd been fast and clever, but honest. He'd tried to buy the black-and-white pinto numerous times, Fargo remembered with a smile. The next time Fargo ran across him, Broken Oak had settled down at the edge of Indian territory, where he'd built a big compound and a big business trading horses, buffalo skins, and trinkets to the Cheyenne, Arapaho, Kiowa, and Comanche. Broken Oak had a Cheyenne wife by then, and a willowy daughter who lurked shyly in the back room. And Broken Oak had upped his bid, offering Fargo a wagonload of goods for the Ovaro. Broken Oak always had a good eye for horseflesh. His trading post had been one of the most successful ventures on the plains.

And yet, the shrewd trader had left the high plains and come to this godforsaken country. Fargo's eyes narrowed as he gazed ahead at the Granite Mountains. It didn't make sense. There wasn't any trade in the middle of the Mojave Desert. No one came into this country. They hadn't passed a single dwelling, ranch, or outpost. Why the hell would Broken Oak have settled here?

Fargo remembered the colonel's words back at Fort Desoto. "They do a helluva business," Colonel Power had said, ". . . trade with the fort all the time."

The colonel had been lying, Fargo realized. Broken Oak didn't trade with the fort. It suddenly struck Fargo that the trail they'd been following toward Broken Oak's Trading Post hadn't been traveled for a long, long time. Yet, Power had wanted him to think the trail was open and well traveled.

Fargo leaned over and absentmindedly stroked the pinto's neck as his thoughts whirled. Colonel Power had lied about Broken Oak. Why? Fargo pulled up short and turned the pinto about. He signaled the men to continue forward as he galloped back down the line. The old sergeant's mule was trotting in the rear. Fargo pulled up next to him.

"Fall back, soldier," Fargo said.

Dade nodded, his eyes wary. The train pulled ahead of them until they walked their mounts, trailing some distance away, well out of earshot.

"What's going on here?" Fargo said roughly.

The sarge shrugged, his eyes questioning.

"Colonel Power told me the fort traded with Broken Oak all the time. But nobody's been on this trail for a long time. Power lied."

Dade laughed bitterly.

"Yeah, he would. We ain't had word of Broken Oak since this trail closed down."

"And when was that?"

"About the time we last heard from Company F. Two years back." The sarge turned in his saddle to look at Fargo full in the face. His eyes, deep sunk, were watchful and full of pain. He spoke bitterly.

"First the colonel sent word to Conrad to come back in. Conrad sent word back. He refused. The colonel sent a second order and the messenger didn't return. So, Power dispatched a campaign party to retrieve him. Sent forty of the best, most seasoned troops." The sarge's voice was edged, hard, and brutal. "There were men who had more experience of this kind of hell than anybody else in the Southwest. And I was supposed to go with them."

The sarge paused and swallowed dry, remembering. "But I was laid up. In the infirmary with a broken ankle."

Dade paused again. Fargo noticed the sergeant's hands gripped tight on the reins, the rough knuckles white.

"You know what happened to those forty men? Not one of them came back. Not a goddamned one. The colonel almost lost his position over that one.

The top brass doesn't take kindly to a troop, a major, and forty men just disappearing with no trace."

Sergeant Dade paused for a moment, his eyes on the distance. The lines deepened around his eyes.

"This was supposed to be empty desert. Whatever is out here killed a troop and then another forty of the army's best men. Got 'em, every single one."

Fargo thought for a moment.

"Colonel Power mentioned something about some Indian renegades in the vicinity."

"Yeah," Dade said with a shrug. "We heard word of some small band hiding out here. Maybe four or five of 'em. Not enough to kill forty of our best men. And Conrad's whole company." Sergeant Dade squinted into the sun, his deep eyes dark. "Whoever, whatever's out there . . ." He left the rest of his thoughts unspoken.

"Did you know the major?" Fargo asked.

"I knew him." Dade's face was hard as a weathered bluff, the lines carved deep. "I knew him. Served under him once. Tough man, hard to please. But at least he knew the country, understood danger. Helluva lot better'n . . ."

"Better than asses like the lieutenant," Fargo finished for him. "Go on."

"I heard he changed after his wife died. Got even tougher. 'Ole Bullet Eyes,' the regulars used to call him."

Fargo thought of the photo he'd seen of Major Conrad, with his hard, angry eyes.

"Why didn't Conrad return to the fort on the colonel's orders? What kept him out there?"

The sarge chewed on his lip a moment as he considered the question.

"He was a tough major," he said at last. "Damn tough. Maybe he just thought he was tougher than this land."

Fargo nodded and then spurred the Ovaro and galloped to the head of the line again. There was another reason, Fargo felt sure. The major had been an experienced army man. He wouldn't have stayed out in the desert if there hadn't been a good reason.

His thoughts were still on Major Conrad as they approached the foot of the Granite Mountains now. The sharp peaks gnawed at the white-hot sky. The few dark piñon pines dotted the northern, cooler folds of the pleated hills. Where the trail led up the barren hillside, the land seemed broken, disturbed. Fargo's keen gaze picked out the rounded shape of an adobe building which blended into the hillside, remaining almost unseen against the rocks and soil.

As they neared, Fargo signaled the men to pull up into defensive position, with Katie riding between the two wagons. He stared at the trading post as they came closer. A high wall of adobe surrounded the place, pierced by a few elongated rifle holes. The adobe was flaking, and numerous bullet holes pitted the mud walls. The area around the post was devoid of plant life—the few pines had been stripped of their branches down to the stump and even the tufts of yellow grass were gone.

A huge wooden door closed off the entrance. Bolted from the inside, Fargo knew.

"Whatdya want?" a man's voice called out. Fargo looked up and saw a rifle barrel poked out of one of the holes in the wall.

"Looking for Broken Oak," Fargo said.

"Who are you?"

There was a flurry of movement beside him as Lieutenant Pike spurred his horse forward impatiently.

"U.S. Army!" Pike shouted. "Open up the door."

A sudden shot was the answer. The lieutenant's hat flew off his head and fluttered to the ground. Pike drew his pistol but Fargo was faster. In an instant, the Colt was in Fargo's hand, speaking fire. The lieutenant's gun was torn out of his fist just as he pulled the trigger. Pike's shot flew wide.

The officer yelped and tucked his right hand beneath his armpit, turning on Fargo in a fury.

"What the hell do you think . . ."

Fargo raised the Colt again, pointing it between the lieutenant's eyes.

"Shut up," he muttered. He turned back toward the looming adobe structure before them.

"Is that you, Broken Oak?"

There was a long silence. Fargo strained his memory to recall the sound of Broken Oak's voice. It was impossible to tell if the hoarse, tired voice belonged to the trader he had known so many years before.

"What do you want?" the voice called out again.

"We're looking for Major Conrad and Company F," Fargo shouted.

"They're dead," the voice answered wearily. "Go back to your fort."

"He's not!" Katie said, spurring her voice forward.

"Get back," Fargo said.

Katie reluctantly obeyed him.

"Who's the girl?"

Fargo didn't like the question, but decided to answer it.

"Conrad's daughter."

Fargo heard a slight rustle inside and the sound of voices—two voices? Arguing.

"And who are *you*?" the voice called out again.

"Name's Fargo. Skye Fargo."

"He's dead, too," the voice replied tiredly. "They're all dead."

"Then where's Broken Oak?" Fargo asked hotly. He'd had enough of this fool's game. He had a sudden inspiration. "Tell Broken Oak that I reconsidered his offer. I've come to sell him my pinto." If it was indeed the old trader, he'd get the joke, Fargo thought.

There was a hoarse laugh from inside the wall. The rifle barrel was pulled inside and Fargo heard movement. The door was being unbolted.

"Stand ready," Fargo said in a low voice to the soldier just behind him. "It may be a trap. Keep your rifles ready and stay alert."

The big wooden door swung open slowly. In the center of a bare dirt yard was a pile of bones, horses, and burros, by the look of them, Fargo noted. And the doors and windows of a small adobe dwelling could be seen on the opposite wall of the enclosure. A small figure stepped around the edge of the door and hurried forward.

She was lithe and dressed in fringed buckskins, her long dark hair in braids which fluttered like birds as she ran. She stopped beside the pinto and laid a hand on its black-and-white neck, then looked up at Fargo.

"I danced to the rain god," she said simply, her almond eyes wide. "And they have sent you."

There was something in the shy way she looked at him from under her lowered lids that brought back to his memory the willowy child hiding behind the flour barrels. Fargo suddenly realized that the woman before him was Broken Oak's daughter. He glanced toward the trading post and saw, leaning in the doorway, the small sinewy shape of Broken Oak, his rifle held across his belly.

"Yes," she said, "I am Summer Lightning." She suddenly glanced around in fear. "But come, quickly. Come inside quickly."

Summer Lightning backed up a few paces.

"Why?" Fargo asked. "What are you afraid of?"

As if on a signal, gunfire erupted from the top of the slope above them. Fargo glanced up to see the dark shapes of horsed men pouring down the sides of the hill. They weren't Indians, but they were too far to see clearly. And still out of rifle range. But in a few moments, their bullets would rain in like hail.

Fargo swore. Summer Lightning shrieked and ran toward the trading post. Broken Oak had disappeared and the large wooden door was starting to close.

3

Summer Lightning was running for her life as the big wooden door was slowly closing and the attackers swooped down the hillside. Fargo hesitated. Was it a trap? Was there an ambush waiting inside the enclosure, too? Fargo hesitated a moment, debating whether to push into the trading post or stand and fight on the open ground. In an instant, he had made up his mind.

The Ovaro leapt forward, galloping hard over the bare ground toward the closing door. Summer Lightning slipped inside and the door was just about shut when Fargo reached it. He pulled his Sharps up and wedged it between the jamb and the thick door. Inside, he heard her voice pleading for the door to be opened.

"Let us in, or we'll all die," he shouted, heaving his shoulder against the heavy door.

The door fell back, opening slowly. Behind him, swarmed the soldiers, the mules protesting the heavy use of spurs, the wagons creaking and the whips lashing loudly. All military discipline was gone as the soldiers pushed and shoved inside. Lieutenant Pike shouted ineffectually in the din, even while he tried to push his way through to safety.

With his rifle in one hand, Fargo leapt from the Ovaro and it trotted inside the enclosure. Fargo turned to help drive the other animals inside. He glanced up at the attackers pouring down the hill. They were close enough now that he could identify them as bandidos, up from Mexico. They wore weather-beaten sombreros, bandoliers of bullets crossed over their chests—and bright silver spurs. There were twenty of them and they were coming on fast.

The first wagon squeezed through the doorway. The mule team of the second wagon suddenly stopped, digging their heels in. Fargo seized the bridle of the lead mule. Sergeant Dade dismounted and grabbed another of the forward mules. Together, they got the team started up again. Fargo dropped the bridle and stood aside as the second wagon swung into the trading post.

Katie rode just behind. The carrot-topped soldier brought up the rear, holding his manacled hands before him. He was fumbling furiously, trying to pull the butt of his rifle up from his saddle holster, his eyes white-rimmed in terror. The pounding hoofs of the approaching horses and the whine of the bullets cut through the hot afternoon air. Suddenly, Katie's chestnut balked and then reared.

Katie screamed but clung to its mane as the horse rose up, screaming with terror. It came down hard and bucked. Katie kept her seat but dropped the reins, which flew up and over the horse's head. Fargo leapt for the chestnut and grabbed the black mane with one hand. His other hand grasped the rifle, which he flung over the saddle horn.

The chestnut took off, heading straight away from the trading post. Katie grabbed the rifle and hung on as Fargo's feet dragged the dust until he pulled himself up, using his powerful arms, and threw one leg over, holding on to the horse's neck. Katie reached her arms around him, one hand holding on to the Sharps. He leaned down, grabbed the reins, which were fluttering wildly, and flung them upward over the horse's head. He pulled the chestnut's nose down hard just as the bullets began to zing around them.

The horse came around bucking and headed back toward the post. Fargo swore and glanced up. The bandidos were approaching the adobe building. The chestnut was galloping full out now, but even so, they would arrive at the front of the trading post barely ahead of the bandidos. The door was nearly closed. The handcuffed kid was kicking his burro in vain. The animal had stopped just short of the entrance, refusing to go in. Above, from the top of the wall and through the long dark slits in the thick adobe, rifles appeared as the soldiers began returning fire. The bandidos' bullets kicked up the dust before them and screamed through the air.

"Keep your head down!" Fargo yelled at Katie. He reached behind him and pulled the Sharps from her grip, raised it, and sighted down the long barrel. One of the bandidos, a skinny black-vested one, had spotted them and veered off his course toward the post to ride straight for them. His carved silver pistols blazed orange and he was shouting in Spanish.

Fargo pulled the trigger. The Sharps rifle kicked back and the bandido spun about in his saddle. He clutched at his shoulder with one hand as he was hurled off his horse. One boot caught in his stirrup and he shrieked as his horse ran wild across the nubby desert and he was dragged along helplessly.

Behind him, Fargo felt Katie slide her rifle from the saddle holster. He squeezed off a second shot as they galloped nearer the entrance. The kid, whose hands had been cuffed by Lieutenant Pike, slid down off the braying burro, who refused to move. He made one last attempt to pull his rifle out of his saddle with his restrained hands and then staggered toward the wooden door. A bullet caught him dead center in the back and he pitched forward, his manacled hands reaching toward the crack in the door and toward safety. Fargo swore as he saw the door begin to close. A few of the men on the top of the wall shouted to them to hurry.

Katie cried out in pain.

"You all right?" he shouted.

She didn't answer, but gripped him tighter around the waist.

The chestnut pulled harder and galloped in, with the bandidos hard on their heels. The bullets rained around them, thudding into the wooden door and pitting the outer layer of adobe. With seconds to spare, the door opened a few feet and Fargo spurred the chestnut forward, forcing it into the narrow opening. The heavy door slammed shut behind them and the bolt shot home.

Inside, the courtyard was chaos, filled with the two wagons, the soldiers running back and forth with rifles and ammunition, and the pile of horses' skeletons. Untethered mules trotted confused and panicked by the whine of the bullets. Fargo slid down immediately and turned back toward Katie Conrad.

"You all right?" he repeated.

Katie wordlessly waved away his question, her face white and her lips tight. Fargo turned and sprinted toward the wall to join the other men.

Outside, the bandidos circled the trading post on their sturdy horses with their high Spanish saddles. They shot their pistols wildly, hardly pausing, screaming and shouting. Their aim wasn't sure, but several of the flying bullets had caught some of the soldiers, who had slumped against the inside of the protecting wall. Fargo fired his Sharps and reloaded again and again. He brought down three men in fast succession. The sergeant, firing beside him, had bagged two.

A portly bandido with a long black mustache drew Fargo's attention. The short man, dressed in black, sat erect on his horse, chest out, his bald head shining in the sun. He stayed to the rear, shooting occasionally, but mainly watching the action as the others dashed in firing. After a few minutes, they withdrew out of range and huddled together.

"They're figuring it ain't worth it," Dade said, taking off his cap and wiping the sweat from his brow.

"But they'll be back," a voice cut in. Fargo

whirled about and looked down. Broken Oak stood there, his brown face cracked with years of hard living, his wiry body angular as a stubborn and ancient tree. Fargo jumped down and seized his arm, shaking the old man roughly.

"You almost got us killed, closing the gate like that," he said. "What the hell's going on here?"

Broken Oak looked up into his face, his deep eyes milky with age and clouded, too, with incomprehension.

"So, Skye Fargo. It *is* you." Broken Oak's eyes seemed to focus more clearly and he repeated the words. The old man was obviously befuddled, Fargo realized. He let go of his arm.

"They wouldn't dare go up against Fort Desoto," Broken Oak said, his smile crooked over his yellow teeth and his eyes never leaving Fargo's face. "Except for the settlers on the trail, this trading post is the only thing worth attacking for a hundred miles. They'll ride away now, but they'll try again in a week or two. Manuel Alvarez never gives up so easily."

"Manuel Alvarez! Fargo climbed onto the parapet and gazed out at the flats. His eyes sought the black-garbed figure again. So that was Alvarez. The bandido's reputation was fierce. He and his band had been terrorizing the southern deserts and northern Mexico for the better part of a decade. As Fargo watched, the bandidos rounded up the spare horses of the dead men and galloped off toward the south.

"Sometimes they wait up in the hills, spying on us, until we venture outside," Broken Oak said.

"Once we have the door open, Alvarez attacks. When he saw you coming with the horses and supplies, I guess he thought he'd get even more."

"Well!" Lieutenant Pike's voice cut in. "It must have been Alvarez who sent that scout to spy on us last night!"

Fargo turned and gave a withering look at the officer. Broken Oak raised his brows quizzically.

"Last night, one of our guards got his throat slit," Fargo explained to Broken Oak. Then he turned to Pike. "But if the Alvarez gang had spotted us, they'd have attacked us long before we approached the post. They'd have ambushed us in the middle of that flat. Or in the middle of the night. Not when we were within running distance to shelter."

Pike's brows furrowed as he tried to think of an answer.

"How many men did we lose?" Fargo asked, his voice hard. Broken Oak watched the two men, looking with interest from one to the other.

"Two," Pike answered. "Not bad."

"Including the one you killed?" Fargo snapped. "The kid you handcuffed so he couldn't get to his rifle when we were attacked?"

"Now, see here!" Pike fairly shouted.

"From now on, I give the orders," Fargo said, "Otherwise, I'll have *you* put in cuffs."

Pike stamped his foot and marched off to issue an unnecessary order about where to tether the mules. Dade, reloading as he kept an eye on the open land, suppressed a smile.

"Why are you way the hell out here?" Fargo asked Broken Oak.

"I ask you the same question," the trader said, his eyes keen now, but evasive. "Come inside and we'll make talk."

As they crossed the yard together, Fargo spotted Summer Lightning's slender buckskin-clad form bending over someone. It was Katie Conrad. He hurried toward them.

Katie sat propped against the wall, her face pale and drawn. Her blue eyes had darkened, like a storm-tossed lake. One leg was stretched out before her on a striped blanket. Blood darkened the colorful wool.

"She took a bullet in the leg," Summer Lightning said, looking up at them. "When she was riding into the fort."

Fargo swore and knelt beside Katie. He gently pulled aside the cotton fabric Summer Lightning used to stanch the blood. A glance told him that Katie had been lucky. Damn lucky. The bullet had passed clean through the muscle of her calf. It was a nasty wound. And she'd have a helluva limp for a long time. But the bullet had missed the artery. She wasn't going to bleed to death. And none of the bones were shattered, so she wouldn't lose her leg either. She'd live and she'd walk. Unless infection got her, of course. Katie moaned and Fargo stroked her cold, sweat-soaked forehead.

"Katie? You hear me?"

Her eyes were almost blind with pain and he wondered if she recognized him. Her lip was bleeding where she'd bit it to keep from crying out and her fists were clenched. Fargo shook his head in amazement. She'd been shot when the chestnut had been racing toward safety, but she hadn't screamed, hadn't fainted. He'd never seen a woman like her.

"What do you have to drink?" Fargo asked.

"Cactus juice. Tequila," Broken Oak said. He walked toward the shelter and returned in a moment with a full bottle of the crystal liquid. Fargo uncorked the bottle and put it to Katie's lips. Her eyes fluttered as she took the first swallow. She gagged and sputtered.

"Swallow," he encouraged. She obeyed and then took a second swig. Fargo put the bottle in her hand. Even though she was half unconscious, Katie had the kind of willful pride that would keep her from wanting to make a sound. He'd seen the trait before, but never in a woman. He glanced again at the wound.

"You got any prickly pear growing around here?" he asked Summer Lightning. She nodded, understanding his thought.

"Yes, up the hill. That would help her."

Fargo left Katie to examine the chestnut. If the bullet had passed through her leg while she'd been riding, it might have wounded the horse. But he found a flattened lead slug embedded in a metal disc on the saddle skirt. Then he climbed onto the parapet again and took a long look from the top of the adobe wall. The long shadows of the hills were now reaching across the barren flat. The sky was brilliant orange. Around the trading post, the land was still. The Alvarez gang had headed south across the flat. It would be worth the risk, Fargo decided.

"If you spot any movement at all," he told the

soldiers keeping watch, "give a warning shot and we'll head back in."

The gate was unbarred and Fargo and Summer Lightning slipped outside. She carried a leather sack and sat behind him on the Ovaro. They galloped up the slope, past the denuded piñon pines.

"Looks like you've stripped almost everything around the fort," Fargo commented.

"Sometimes Alvarez has camped up on the hilltop for a week or so, waiting for us to give up. We can never be sure if he is there or not. Sometimes he is gone for months. Then he camps there for weeks at a time. During those times, I sneak out at night to get some nuts or more wood. They do not watch so well at night."

"Why don't you and Broken Oak get the hell out of here?"

Summer Lightning stiffened behind him and did not answer. They were hiding something, damn it. But what?

Fargo kept a sharp lookout, even though he was fairly certain Alvarez had not doubled back. As they cut on a diagonal, ascending the barren slope, Fargo thought over her words. Now he was certain that whoever had spied their camp the night before hadn't been from Alvarez's band.

Fargo spotted the flat green cactus dotting the hillside and they dismounted. Using the knife from his ankle holster, Fargo bent down and began cutting some of the discs, holding them delicately, careful not to get the spines in his fingers.

"Why did Broken Oak come here?" Fargo suddenly asked her, hoping to catch her off guard.

Summer Lightning's eyes widened for a moment and a dark look of fear flashed through them. Then she hooded her eyes as if she had revealed too much and looked away.

"Ask my father."

"Where's your mother? I didn't see her in the compound."

Summer Lightning slowly drew a long knife from her belt. Then she turned her shoulder to him, bent over, and began to harvest the ruddy cactus fruit. Fargo held the leather bag open as she dropped them inside. Her buckskin dress inched up her strong brown thighs. Each time she bent over, Fargo saw her long breasts with their dark nipples, swaying as the neckline of her dress gaped open.

"She died," Summer Lightning said after a long time. "Please don't ask me questions. For my father, everyone is dead," she answered. She straightened up suddenly and walked back to the Ovaro, mounting it without a backward glance. They rode back to the trading post in silence.

When they arrived, Summer Lightning disappeared around one side of the adobe shelter. Several of the soldiers stood guard and the others had lit a fire and were cooking dinner in the courtyard. Katie lay in the same spot, her eyes heavy and the tequila bottle half empty. Fargo skinned the cactus pads and applied them as poultices on either side of Katie's wound, binding them with lengths of cotton. The cactus flesh would draw out the fluids of the bullet wound, while the juices would dull the pain. Katie's head lolled to one side as he picked her up in his arms. He carried her toward the small adobe shelter.

Summer Lightning bent over a small oven. She glanced up and gestured toward the low doorway. Fargo carried Katie inside, passing through the large main room and ducking through a doorway. In this smaller room, he deposited her on one of the rope beds against the wall. Her eyelids were drooping. He sat beside her as she took another swig from the tequila bottle, and then took it from her fist as she fell asleep.

The main room was whitewashed, the walls bare except for shelves of pottery and baskets. A rude table and chairs stood beside one of the windows. Broken Oak leaned against a bare white wall, smoking a fragrant herb. He avoided Fargo's eyes.

"Now we'll talk," Fargo said.

Broken Oak shrugged, his cracked face impassive. The old man's eyes were lucid, but he refused to speak.

"Cut the bullshit," Fargo spat.

Broken Oak sighed and pursed his lips. After a long silence, he began, his half whisper hoarse and wavering.

"I remember you, Skye Fargo. Summer Lightning remembers you. Even my wife, Silver Wing, remembered you. Fargo was a good man, we always said, when we remembered you."

Broken Oak paused to refill his pipe. Then he offered it to Fargo, who took it and smoked slowly, waiting patiently for Broken Oak to get to the point. Broken Oak was a half-breed, but he'd always had more of the Indian ways about him. Especially the way of saying everything important by taking as much time as possible. The part of Fargo that was Indian understood this, too. He could wait.

"My father was Cheyenne," Broken Oak said. "My mother was white. But my brother was full-blood by an Apache slave. Angry brother. Always angry. Did many bad things up on the plains. Our people drove him away. One day I got a pain in my side like fire." Broken Oak put his hand to his ribs. "This pain did not go away and soon I could not move. I knew the pain would kill me soon. The medicine man told me I must go to find my brother. Then the pain would stop. So, I came."

"So, where is this brother?" Fargo asked.

Broken Oak gestured out beyond the encircling wall.

"Crowheart's band lives out there," he said.

Fargo felt a cold wave pass through him at the name.

"Crowheart?" he said, disbelieving. "But he's been dead for years." Fargo remembered the story of the famous Indian renegade, the most notorious, bloodthirsty killer in the West. Crowheart had raped and carved up dozens of women and children for five years until finally a federal marshal tracked him down. When Crowheart was hanged in Denver City six years before, the engraving of the execution had been on the front page of every newspaper in the West.

Broken Oak shook his head. "It was one of his men, wearing Crowheart's clothes," Broken Oak said. "Crowheart is slippery as a fox. Nobody knew his face. And the real Crowheart escaped from jail. He is here."

"And your brother is with him?" Fargo asked.

"Crowheart *is* my brother," Broken Oak said.

Fargo leaned against the wall next to Broken Oak, his eye unseeing as his thoughts stirred in him. Crowheart. His name brought back the details of the sadistic killings sprayed across the West. And Crowheart had a talent for attracting the most violent misfits and desperados. A dozen times the outlaw had been hunted down and captured, but always, at the last instant, he slipped away before being brought to justice. And when they had hanged him, or thought they had, there had been a celebration in Denver City that lasted for days. Fargo shook his head slowly at the thought of how the news would be received that Crowheart was still alive, hiding out in the Mojave Desert after all these years.

Crowheart's presence in the Mojave explained the disappearance of Major Conrad and Company F. It also explained how forty of Fort Desoto's best men could have been lost without a trace. But nothing explained why Major Conrad would have ignored his orders to abandon Fort Chingo and return to the relative safety of Colonel Power's command post. Something drove Conrad to remain out in this empty hell, but Fargo was stumped as to what it could be. It was crazy. About as crazy as Broken Oak following his renegade brother out here.

"So you see," Broken Oak said, his clouded eyes watching Fargo's face as if he could read every thought, "this is my fate. My brother knows I am here. Every few months, I see him riding, alone, on the ridge of the hills. But he never comes."

"It's not your fate to sit here and die," Fargo said. "You should get the hell out. Think of Summer Lightning."

"It's too late," Broken Oak said. "All my horses died. If I try to go on foot, Alvarez and his men will get us for sure. No, it is over. Everything is over."

Fargo stood for a while looking down on the wiry trader, whose face was as creased and dry as the rain-cut desert around them. He'd seen men lose their spirits before. Sometimes it came back. Sometimes.

"Did you know Major Conrad?" he asked. At least he could pry some information out of the old man.

"Good leader," Broken Oak said with a nod. "I knew him when he took over the fort in Kansas on Arrowpoint Water." Fargo remembered that was what the Indians called the Arkansas River. "But many of the Indians were angry because the big chief before Conrad killed many of our people. My brother, Crowheart ..."

Broken Oak took a long, thoughtful drag on his pipe.

"Crowheart blamed all the white men for the murder of his Apache mother. He wanted to kill the big army chief, Conrad, so he hunted him. But Conrad was too smart and there were too many soldiers. Crowheart could not find a way to hurt Conrad and finally, my people drove Crowheart away."

How strange, Fargo thought, that Crowheart and Major Conrad should have ended up together again in the Mojave Desert. If Crowheart had vowed revenge on Major Conrad in particular, then there was no chance Conrad would have survived. But he had promised Colonel Power he would go all the way to Fort Chingo to have a look. And Katie Conrad would never rest easy until she knew for certain that her father was dead.

Fargo was quiet for the rest of the evening as he thought about the best plan of action. With Crowheart and his band lurking about and Alvarez and his bandidos on the rampage, it didn't make sense to take Katie all the way to Fort Chingo. It was two hard days' ride from the trading post anyway. He would leave her with Summer Lightning and Broken Oak, along with a few of the men, in the safety of the adobe walls. Then, he would lead a party on the fastest mules to make a fast run up to the fort. That way, they could travel light, without the wagons.

Summer Lightning served them warm Indian fry bread, beans, and the cactus fruit, which she had roasted over the fire to singe off the fuzz. All during the meal, she watched Fargo thoughtfully. When they had finished eating, Fargo checked on Katie. She was sleeping fitfully on the bed, knocked out by the tequila, but he was glad to see she wasn't feverish. Fargo changed the cactus poultices. He spent some time inspecting the soldiers who were patrolling the top of the perimeter wall. Then he fetched the bedroll from the Ovaro and looked about for a comfortable resting place.

A rough-hewn ladder leaned against the wall of the adobe building. Fargo climbed up it and found the flat rooftop was surrounded by a high wall, cutting off the view from the soldiers on the top of the wall. Overhead, the moonless sky dome was crowded with stars. A cool desert wind blew steadily from the west and the singing of the coyotes carried for miles over the otherwise silent land.

He had laid out the bedroll when he heard someone climbing up the ladder behind him. He turned around as Summer Lightning reached the top and swung a long brown leg over the low wall surrounding the roof. Fargo walked toward her, his hand outstretched, to help her over. She smiled at him, her dark eyes quiet and desiring. Just as she swung over her second leg, he pulled her toward him and took her in his arms. Neither of them spoke a word. There was no need to.

She came, eagerly, hungrily, her mouth open to his deep kisses. He ran his big hands up and down her narrow back as she arched against him, warm and soft, her large breasts like pillows between them. He plunged his tongue between her sweet lips and she flicked it with hers, purring low in her throat like a cat. He felt himself harden, engorged with desire for her, aching to be deep between her legs.

She guided his hand between them, toward her breast. He slipped inside the buckskin dress and felt the fullness of her in the palm of his hand. He kneaded the tight nipple between his fingers as he inhaled the herb essence of her hair and tongued her ear.

"Oh, oh," she whispered. "For so many years, I thought of you, I thought of tonight." She reached down and inched her dress upward until it was bunched up around her waist and she undulated against him. Fargo released her and moved toward the ladder, pulling it up behind him. When he turned back, Summer Lightning stood before him, naked under the moonlight.

She was beautiful, dark, and slim, her large hanging breasts brown-tipped over her narrow rib cage and waist. Between her muscular thighs, the small triangle of fur glistened. Summer Lightning smiled and reached up, loosening her hair, which cascaded around her like a dark waterfall. She turned and Fargo admired the tight, round buttocks as she walked across the roof and lay down on his bedroll.

Fargo walked toward her as he removed his shirt. He felt her eyes on his broad muscular chest as he got out of his boots and unbuttoned his jeans. He stripped and stood above her as her gaze lingered on his huge erection. Summer Lightning purred softly and spread her legs enticingly, cupping her own breasts and lifting them upward toward him. He lowered himself onto her, taking one breast, then the other, into his mouth and teasing the nipples between his teeth gently.

Summer Lightning gasped, her hips thrusting upward, seeking his hard shaft. Her slick wetness rubbed against him. Fargo lifted himself upward, positioning the tip of his hardness just at her entrance. She looked at him wide-eyes as he waited for a long moment, and then slowly entered her, savoring the hot embrace of her around his engorged penis. She let out a slow gasp as he lay on her, fully inside her.

She murmured in Algonquian. Fargo began to thrust, slowly at first, his hands kneading her heavy breasts as he plunged fully into her, faster and then faster. He reached down and grabbed her tight buttocks, pulling her upward as he pushed harder. She panted, tossing her head from side to side, her eyes unfocused. Fargo felt her contractions, deep within her, squeezing him rhythmically. His penis grew larger as the heat gathered at the base of him.

She was muttering now, clawing at his back in ecstasy, as he thrust to one side and then the other. She suddenly stiffened all over, then cried out, stifling the sound against his shoulder as she came, pushing upward to meet him. Just as his balls tightened and he felt the explosion gathering in him, she reached around and thrust one finger up his ass.

Fargo's cock became a red hot fountain, spewing inside of her tightness as he rode her, thrusting and coming, again and again, racked by the orgasmic contractions, until he was spent. Fargo slowed, still moving inside her slipperiness, but slowly, until finally, he stopped and rolled off her. She cuddled up to him, still breathing hard.

"It was even better than I imagined. . . ." she murmured, her hand trailing across his chest. Fargo held her in his arms until he heard her breathing slow as she slipped into sleep. He lay for a long time looking up at the circling stars.

His thoughts turned to the men he was leading. Soldiers he was responsible for. Two men shot in the fight with Alvarez. One handcuffed kid gunned down unnecessarily. One jumped by an unknown night visitor. Four down. That left only eight and Lieutenant Pike. Pike was useless. Worse than useless.

Once they left the trading post, the soldiers would face the worst kind of hell in their military career. He'd need to figure out which ones he could completely count on. Fargo thought of each of the men, going over what he had observed.

Sergeant Dade, the old soldier, was completely dependable. If only he had a troop of men like him. And the kid, Tommy Gibbons, was green, but obedient and fast. The other men were surly and undisciplined for the most part. And then there was Billy Sullivan. Fargo thought of the man's ruddy, angry face and loud voice. He was a troublemaker for sure.

And that was the troop he had to get across the hottest, driest tract in the Southwest to find Fort Chingo. And maybe fight Alvarez and Crowheart on the way. Stupid job, Fargo thought. Goddamned lousy assignment. He turned over and went to sleep.

The next morning, Fargo arose at dawn and dressed quietly without waking Summer Lightning, who lay curled naked on the bedroll. Fargo smiled, remembering the night before and anticipating another night with her. The troop would stay another day at the trading post to rest up and prepare for the last dash to Fort Chingo.

Fargo had already decided which of the soldiers would stay behind the walls of the trading post while he led the rest on a quick ride to reconnoiter the fort. But the first order of business was to inspect all the supplies and figure out what to take. He hoisted the ladder over the edge of the rooftop and climbed down into the courtyard.

Most of the soldiers lay wrapped in their blankets. Two were on duty, walking slowly around the top of the encircling adobe wall. The fat cook stood by the supply wagon, feeding sticks to a growing campfire. Fargo walked over just as the cook heaved a big keg out of the wagon and began prying off the top.

"Goddamn it," the cook muttered as the top popped off. "More bad pork." He stuck a long knife into the keg and fished out a long slice of rancid pork, covered with green mold. Even from the distance of several feet, the smell was terrible.

"What do you mean, *more* bad pork?" Fargo asked, coming up to them. The cook shrugged helplessly and the sarge shot him a tired glance.

"This is the last keg of pork," the cook said.

"That can't be," said Fargo. "We had enough supplies for the whole trip. Where's the rest of it?"

"Gone bad, too," the cook said. "For every keg I opened, one of 'em was rotten. Beans, too. Thick with black slime."

Fargo swore and stepped forward to look in the supply wagon. There were only three kegs left now. Not nearly enough food, even if they were all right. He whirled about and grabbed the cook's shirt collar, hauling the fat man up close.

"Why the hell didn't you tell me sooner?" Fargo spat at him.

The cook's face turned white and his mouth gaped.

"Well, the first couple of kegs were fine. Then, when I got further into the wagon, they got bad. I ... I reported it to Lieutenant Pike. Honest, sir. He said rotten food wasn't very important but he'd tell you. But I guess he didn't ..."

"That goddamned idiot," Fargo said, releasing the cook. "Of course he didn't tell me!"

Lieutenant Pike wasn't fit for duty, Fargo thought again. The officer was a blowhard, a bad leader who had never been on campaign outside a fort. He was helpless and hopeless. Pike hadn't even raised an alarm about the bad supplies. And now they were going to run out of food before they even got to Fort Chingo. The cook pried off a top of one of the remaining kegs of beans. Inside, the dried beans were covered with a layer of black putrid ooze.

"That figures," muttered the cook.

"What figures?" Fargo asked.

"Colonel Power didn't send any of the army's edible food with us," the cook said. "I guess he figured, what's the point of sending good supplies on a suicide mission?"

The cook swallowed hard, and his voice was cracked with fear.

"We're all going to die, aren't we?"

4

"I don't plan on dying," Fargo snapped at the fat cook. "And I don't want to hear any more talk like that. Get these barrels open and give me a report on what's left. And get a move on!"

Fargo spun on his heels and stalked away. That's all he needed—bad morale. On a rough campaign, it only took one scared soldier to infect a whole troop. He spotted Summer Lightning climbing down the ladder just as Broken Oak emerged from the low door of the adobe dwelling. His eyes were clear today, Fargo noted, with no sign of the confusion of the day before. The old trader seemed exactly like the man Fargo had met so many years before.

"I rested well," Broken Oak said with a smile and a twinkle. "Once the thumping on the roof stopped." Summer Lightning shot a wide smile at Fargo and playfully slapped her father's arm as she disappeared into the house. "She has often talked about you," the old man said to Fargo, his watery eyes looking after her. "She was only a young girl, but you took her heart away."

"She's a fine woman," Fargo said.

All around the yard, the soldiers stirred and rolled out of their blankets. Lieutenant Pike emerged from the tent pitched in one corner, his brass buttons gleaming. He spotted Fargo and headed toward him, rubbing his hands together.

"Well! I'll muster a formal roll call this morning," the lieutenant said enthusiastically. "And then we'll saddle up and head out to Fort Chingo."

"No, we don't," Fargo replied. "We rest up a day and get everything in order. Then, *you* are staying here with Broken Oak to guard the women. I'm taking some of the men for a fast ride to Fort Chingo and back."

"But, but . . ."

"Shut up, Pike!" exploded Fargo. "You don't know what the hell you're doing out here! You handcuff a kid for wearing the wrong boots and he gets himself shot because he can't get to his rifle! You issue orders to pitch a tent where a flash flood will wash it downstream! And you completely ignore the fact that we're running out of supplies! You're the worst example of a head-up-his-ass incompetent officer that I've ever seen!"

Lieutenant Pike's mouth gaped open several times like a fish and he swallowed hard. Several of the men nearby stifled their sniggering. The lieutenant whirled about and marched off, disappearing into the tent. Fargo wondered if he'd have more trouble with him or if the lieutenant would finally back down.

"Come inside," Broken Oak said. "I have something interesting to show you." Fargo followed the old man inside and to a small corner cupboard.

The old trader reached inside and pulled out a thin packet of folded papers, tied with a bit of jute string. "Letters from Major Conrad," the old man said. "When the riders from Fort Desoto stopped coming, I still sometimes traded with Fort Chingo. At least for a while. These letters were addressed to his daughter." Broken Oak nodded toward the door where Katie lay. Fargo took the letters and went into the other room.

Katie Conrad lay on the bed, her face flushed, her sleep uneasy. He touched her forehead, which was hot and dry with a slight fever. Fargo spent some time changing the cactus pads on her wound. She hardly stirred. Then he washed up and sat down at the table to read the letters from Conrad. Maybe in them he would find a clue to what had happened at Fort Chingo. He flipped through them and then chose the last one, with a date just the previous year.

"My dearest Katie," the letter began. "He is everywhere, night and day. Up Rio Chingo. But I will find him. And then I will wrap him in a blanket of death, like he did my dear departed Ann, your mother. He will writhe and scream in agony, sweating and stinking, in his blanket. Or maybe I will show him mercy and I will cut his throat very slowly, letting him bleed. The men are afraid. Some have run away. They are cowards but I do not need them. I only need this blanket. And my friend, death, will help me . . .

Fargo put the letter down slowly. Major Conrad had obviously gone stark-raving mad. What the hell was all this about "he?" And the blanket? Fargo riffled through some of the other letters, reading sentences here and there, but they were all the same, ravings about someone who seemed to be haunting the fort. Fargo thought of Alvarez and his *bandidos*. Or perhaps it was Crowheart. Then there were the numerous references to a blanket or the blanket of death. And a blanket that had killed Ann, the major's wife. None of that made any sense.

For a few minutes, Fargo considered returning to Fort Desoto. There wasn't a chance in the world that Major Conrad was still alive out there. In his hand, Fargo held evidence that the man had lost his mind. He couldn't have lived, insane, in the desert for two years.

But Fargo had said he would go up Rio Chingo to the fort. That had been the agreement. And, even with the bandidos and the renegades around, he knew he had to do it. There was something tugging on him, something that was pulling him toward that lonely outpost which lay at the top of the dry, winding riverbed. It was as if he, too, had to see it with his own eyes. He had to know what had happened.

The rest of the day passed quickly. The cook reported that there was one good keg of beans left and one bag of flour, once he'd strained the worms out of it. There was a little hardtack and some beef jerky. Fargo sent several forays of men out to gather piñon nuts and more prickly pear fruit to supplement the meager stores. If he put the men on half rations, he decided, they'd just have enough. Broken Oak's trading post had a deep well and they refilled all their canteens and watered the live-stock well.

Fargo spent an hour currying the pinto's black-and-white coat. He watered the horse, fed it the best oats, and checked its hooves for loose stones. The desert heat was hell on horses, Fargo knew. The pinto was strong, stronger than any horse he'd ever seen. Still, the days ahead would tax the Ovaro's strength.

The soldiers who weren't gathering food spent time cleaning their weapons, taking care of the mules, and keeping guard. Pike sulked around his tent. At sunset, Fargo went to check again on Katie Conrad. She was sitting up now, her face still flushed, her long auburn hair spread out on the pillow. Katie's blue eyes were dark worry when she looked up. Her father's letters were scattered about her on the bed.

"He ... he's gone crazy, hasn't he?"

Fargo nodded and watched as she wiped away the tears.

"We're leaving tomorrow morning," Fargo said. "You're not well enough to ride yet. I'll be back in four days to tell you what I find at Fort Chingo. In the meanwhile, you rest."

Katie nodded mutely. She reached out and took his hand, then pressed it to her cheek.

"I wanted to go all the way to the fort," Katie said. "If you find him alive, would you tell him that? Even if he doesn't understand, please tell him that."

"If he's alive," Fargo said. He stood looking down at her for a long moment. She was beautiful.

Her pale blue eyes were fringed with long lashes and her cheeks were flushed. She smiled up at him and he realized how much she had been on his mind, almost without his knowing.

Fargo bent over and kissed her, softly, swiftly. Katie reached her hands up to grasp him behind the neck as he nuzzled her neck. She smelled of lavender. He stood to leave.

"Thank you. For everything," Katie said. He smiled down at her. Just four days, he told himself. Four days and he'd be back and her leg would be better. He left quickly, not trusting himself not to linger.

He was lying out under the cold stars, wrapped in his bedroll and thinking of Katie Conrad when he heard Summer Lightning climbing up the ladder. She pulled up the ladder after her, tiptoed across the rooftop, paused to strip off her buckskin dress, and slid in beside him. She was warm and silky, her nakedness smooth against him. He moved his hands gratefully over her slender taut body. He felt himself grow hard as he explored her, more slowly than the night before, less urgently.

"We are not alone," Summer Lightning said sadly, as he was making his way down her torso, kissing, licking, exploring. "You are thinking of another." Fargo paused and felt her stiffen slightly, waiting for his reply.

"I was," he said. "That is true. But I am thinking only of you now." Summer Lightning relaxed beneath him as he began kissing her again, going lower until he inhaled her musky odor and took her folded lips into his mouth, teasing and sucking until she moaned and cried out in total abandon. And then he took her again, under the stars, entering her with such sudden ferocity that they both cried out. And as she opened wider, taking him into her as deeply as was possible, he could not possibly have thought of anyone but the lithe and warm woman, Summer Lightning, who welcomed him inside her.

Dawn blazed white hot. The six soldiers stood at attention with the best of the mules loaded with four days' supplies. The Ovaro stamped, impatient to be gone.

Lieutenant Pike paced up and down beside his tent. Fargo knew that the lieutenant was secretly relieved to stay behind. He'd sulked and blustered about being left behind, but he hadn't pressed the matter with Fargo. And, Fargo remembered, when the bandidos had attacked, it had been Lieutenant Pike who had pushed himself to the front of the line to try to get into the trading post first. Besides being a bad officer, the man was lily-livered. And if there was one thing they didn't need on the way to Fort Chingo, it was a coward.

As Fargo saddled the pinto, he reviewed his plan. Pike and the cook and a skinny nervous private would stay behind at Broken Oak's trading post. Fargo had even considered leaving the loud-mouthed Billy Sullivan, but in the end, when he thought of the bandidos and Crowheart, he decided he'd need every good gun he could get. And Billy Sullivan could shoot. Sergeant Dade, Tommy Gibbons, and three other men rounded out the party he would lead to Fort Chingo.

Fargo mounted the Ovaro. Summer Lightning and Broken Oak opened the gates. He rode out, followed by the soldiers. The sun, still low in the east, was already blazing hot. It was going to be a scorcher.

They rode all morning without pause, climbing up the winding trail through the Granite Mountains. The sun glittered on the white streaks of alkali which scored the hills that rose up around them. The iron-red rocks gave off waves of heat. Fargo kept the men riding in a tight knot, rifles at the ready. He kept his eyes on the sharp outlines of the slopes above them, but he saw nothing moving. Then, at noon, when the sun was straight overhead and the shadows had disappeared, he realized they were being watched.

They were riding through a narrow culvert between towering sandstone formations. The mules, loping fast, kicked the white dust into the air. Fargo had just turned around to check on the men behind him when he spotted movement against the sky. Just a flicker of something that was there and then gone. From under the shadowy brim of his hat, Fargo's keen eyes swept the rocky slope, but he couldn't discern anything there. But he knew. Somewhere, high above them, riding or walking along the top of the hills, someone was following.

Fargo said nothing. He knew better than to react. Whoever it was might still be watching. He turned back around in the saddle wondering if it was Alvarez and his gang. Or Crowheart. It was only another ten miles to Echo Canyon. Beyond that lay the wide, dry, nameless lake and then the mouth of Rio Chingo. They'd find a good, defensible camp somewhere, Fargo thought. Up against some canyon wall or at the top of a bluff.

They had gone another mile when Fargo heard something, the distant sound of one rock striking another, a sound so soft, another man might not have heard it above the creak of the saddles and the clopping of the hooves on the trail. But Fargo heard it. And what was more, he heard its direction, off to the left, up the slope. Fargo turned away from the sound and gestured for Dade to ride forward alongside him. Just as the man was about to pull up on his mule, Fargo shifted the pinto so Dade could some up alongside his left.

"What's up?" the sergeant asked.

Fargo turned toward Dade as if to talk to him, but his eyes searched the hillside beyond the sarge.

"You see something?" the sarge asked, starting to turn and look.

"Don't," Fargo admonished. "Yeah. I heard something. And I see something, too. We're being watched."

Dade nodded slowly.

"There's one up on the hillside," said Fargo. His sharp gaze had picked out the dark dome of a man's scalp protruding just a little from behind a boulder on a slope of tumbled rocks. As he watched, it slowly sank and disappeared. "He's a damn good tracker. And there's another on our rear."

"Should we pull up in fighting position?" Dade asked.

"No. I don't want to let on we've spotted them. Just bring up the rear. We'll camp early. It might be a long night."

Two hours later, they came to the top of the trail that led down from the sun-blasted rocks into the deep and shadowy Echo Canyon and to the flat alkali land beyond. In the cloudless sky above, the midafternoon sun was like molten gold burning the broken landscape. Fargo reined in and gave the signal for a halt. There was a smudge against the bright sky. Fargo shaded his eyes against the sun's glare and squinted. Yes, a smudge. Smoke rising. About a mile off, from deep in the canyon. Dade came up alongside him.

"More visitors?" he asked.

Fargo pointed wordlessly. They sat for a long moment as Fargo considered every possibility. Two trackers had followed them through the mountains. And now they saw somebody's camp up ahead. Was it a trap? It would make damn good sense, luring them down into the deep canyon and then attacking from all sides.

"Might be an ambush," Fargo said quietly. He scanned the nearby slopes and spotted a short cliff, half in the shade, easy to defend. "You and the men take a rest over there," Fargo said. "I'll go on alone and scout out that fire."

Dade nodded and gave the orders.

"Why the hell are we stopping here?" Billy Sullivan grumbled. "If there's a camp ahead, let's all go and see who the hell it is. I could use some grub." Several of the other men nodded sullenly.

Without a backward glance, Fargo spurred the pinto forward. The strong horse plunged surefootedly down the rocky slope into the shadows. Yard by yard, the path descended and the gray-streaked rocks rose higher around them. The narrow path wound downward, alongside a dry streambed. When he figured he'd gone about halfway to the campfire, Fargo dismounted and left the Ovaro untethered in a shallow culvert. He went forward on foot, quietly, his Colt in hand. The rocky canyon twisted back and forth, airless and hot, but deep in shadow. He crept from rock to rock, keeping cover in case someone came around a bend.

Soon he smelled woodsmoke, then cooking—beans maybe? The men's voices sounded like a babbling brook. He dashed from his rock cover forward to a cleft between a cliff and a huge boulder and peered through. Beyond, the canyon opened out to form a natural circle. Horses were tethered near him and on the far side of the enclosure stood a group of men, all laughing uproariously. Fargo picked out the portly figure of Manuel Alvarez. The bandido shook his fist and shouted something in Spanish which Fargo was too far away to make out. The voice of Alvarez broke like a wave on the rocks of the canyon and poured back to him, echo upon echo. The bandidos laughed again, their voices shattered by the rocks above them and reflected in echoing waves. They passed around a bottle.

Fargo gazed about, his eyes sweeping the broken

rock slopes above the campsite. The bandidos had one guard posted. He was sitting on a rock near the horse, pistol in one hand, bottle in the other.

Fargo backed slowly away and retraced his steps thoughtfully as he formulated his plan. It was almost too good to be true. Alvarez and his gang were in the perfect spot to be attacked—relaxed and half drunk, completely vulnerable. Seemingly. Fargo teased out the possibility that someone from Alvarez's gang had been following them. And that the bandidos were only pretending to be off guard while waiting for an attack. No. It didn't fit, somehow. If they were expecting a fight, they would have camped in a less dangerous position. Fargo turned a corner and spotted the shallow culvert before him where he had left the Ovaro. It was empty.

He stopped, puzzled, Colt still in hand. Then he walked forward, his eyes on the rocky ground. No footprints on bare rock, he thought ruefully. He looked about slowly, measuring the steep slopes of the winding canyon. There was no place the horse could have gone, unless it had sprouted wings. The Ovaro must have retraced its steps to Dade and the waiting men. The pinto had never wandered off before, Fargo thought. He was tempted to whistle for the horse, but he didn't want to chance alerting the Alvarez gang. Fargo swore to himself and continued on foot, keeping an eye out.

On the way back toward the waiting men, Fargo spotted a few side canyons he hadn't noticed before, but they were so narrow, he doubted the horse would have entered them. Finally, he climbed up the last rise. Billy Sullivan sat in the shade, his shirt off and his big gut overhanging his belt buckle. Dade stood with a few of the other men at the top of the trail, rifle in hand. Dade looked relieved to see Fargo.

"Where's your pinto?"

Fargo swore. The horse had not come out of the canyon this way, which meant it had wandered into one of the narrow side canyons. It didn't make sense. Fargo turned back toward the distant rising smoke and decided to take a chance. He puckered his lips and whistled, a distinctive sound which carried for long distances. He paused and waited. He heard nothing. Well, there was no time to lose if they were going to attack. He'd have to run down the Ovaro later.

Fargo gave the orders swiftly and the men mounted. Fargo led the way on foot down into the canyon. When they came to the shallow culvert, the men dismounted. Fargo's thoughts were with the Ovaro. He thought uneasily of the unknown trackers following them and wondered if the pinto had been spirited away. He didn't like it. Not one bit. He designated one of the privates—a tow-headed kid who was nevertheless a good shot—to remain behind, guarding the mules. Then he took his Sharps rifle and plenty of ammunition and gave the rest of the men the instructions for deployment.

The soldiers spent the next hour climbing up the rocks and slowly easing into positions along both sides of the rocky canyon, painstakingly moving from cover to cover until they were looking down from on high into the dark campsite where Alvarez and his men lolled about the yellow fire. Fargo had just taken cover between two boulders when Tommy Gibbons eased up beside him.

"When do we start shooting?" the kid whispered, his hands tight on his rifle.

"In a minute," Fargo said, his eyes on the side of the canyon where three soldiers were snaking along toward the lip of a crumbling bluff.

"There's more of them bandits than there are of us," Tommy said, worriedly. Fargo smiled slowly.

"Echoes," he said. "The echoes will even things out. Once we start firing, that gang won't have a clue where we are."

Fargo's brows lowered as he watched Billy Sullivan and another soldier sprint in full view of the bandidos from one rock to the next. Billy, skirting a slope of scree, stumbled on a rock and it started to roll. Fargo swore as one side of the loose scree started to slide down the slope with a sickening noise that echoed around the canyon. Billy, off balance, waved his arms in the air and the second man reached out to give him a hand.

Down below, the bandidos heard the sound of falling rocks and they jumped to their feet, drew their pistols, and looked wildly about, trying to locate the direction of the sound.

"Shoot. Now!" Fargo shouted. In a moment, the canyon was filled with the resounding pop of gunfire, exploding and echoing off the broken rocks. Fargo spotted Alvarez, sprinting for cover, and aimed for him, dead center. He squeezed the trigger and the Sharps rifle exploded. Alvarez staggered, winged, and fell down behind a rock. Fargo glanced up to see Billy Sullivan, exposed to fire on the rocky slope, had grabbed the other soldier, who had offered his hand. The soldier was full of holes, bleeding. Sullivan was half dragging the man's body as a shield as he inched his way toward cover. Fargo swore. He'd looked away from Sullivan for just an instant, so he hadn't seen what had happened. But it looked like Sullivan had sacrificed somebody else to save himself. Fargo turned his attention back to the fight.

The soldiers were pouring bullets down into the rocky canyon. The sound of the firing was deafening, the echoes bouncing around as the bullets ricocheted. The bandidos crouched helplessly behind rocks to shoot one way, only to find bullets coming from behind them. It was hopeless and they knew it. Fargo picked off one dashing from behind a rock toward the horses, catching him first in the shoulder and spinning him around, and then plugging him full in the gut before he went down.

The horses, maddened by the gunfire and the smell of blood, whinnied and pulled at their pickets. One, a sinewy coyote dun, broke loose and galloped straight through the center of camp. Just then, Alvarez popped up for a second from behind a rock, shooting at the rocks above. The bandido was crouching between two rocks, almost safe from the fusillade. But not safe from ricochets, Fargo thought. He raised the Sharps, calculating where to put a bullet that would bounce into the space between the two rocks, when the horse wheeled about and came close to where Alvarez was hiding.

With a flying leap, the bandido mounted the

horse, his bad arm hanging loose. The bullets, ricocheting off the rocks, caught the horse. One hit its broad chest and it screamed, agonized, and faltered. Alvarez hunched down and beat the horse. A second shot caught the flank. The horse stumbled, but kept its feet as it headed out of the canyon and disappeared behind a rock. There were only three bandits left down below, all wounded and firing only occasionally from behind the rocks. Fargo swore. Alvarez would not get away now.

Fargo bent double and raced along, jumping from side to side, along the top of the cliff, in the direction Alvarez had gone. The three bandidos below caught sight of him and shouted in fury. Fargo wove from side to side, leaping from one rock to the next, in a jerky motion, as the bullets whizzed about him. He felt a white hot pain on his left shoulder as a bullet grazed him, just as he threw himself behind a rock and crawled over the edge of a tall formation.

From here, Fargo could look down into the next bend of the deep canyon. At the rocky bottom, the wounded dun had stopped and Alvarez sat on its back, beating it mercilessly. The horse refused to go. As Fargo watched, the dun's legs crumpled. Fargo brought up his Sharps and took slow aim at the horse's head. It was out of its misery before it hit the ground.

Alvarez jumped off the horse before it collapsed. He rolled to the ground and took cover in a small depression, behind the hulk of dead horse. Fargo swore. Alvarez was too low to get a clear shot. The bandido could hold out for a long while, unless

Fargo could get around the other side of him. But that meant racing from cover. And then Alvarez would know where he was.

He glanced up and saw a sheer-sided formation that made it impossible for him to stay up high and get around to where he could get a clear shot at Alvarez. The only chance, without completely retracing his steps, was to descend the rocky slope below him on a diagonal toward an outcropping, which would give him an angle into the backside of the dead horse, where Alvarez cowered. Fargo plotted his course, rock to rock, then gathered his feet under him.

He sprang from cover and raced, bent double, toward a humpbacked boulder, smashing into it, just as a bullet split the air.

"Give up, Alvarez!" Fargo shouted in Spanish. His words split and echoed.

"Go to hell!" the bandit replied in English. Fargo smiled to himself. The goddamned bastard would go down fighting. So be it.

Fargo made another dash and again Alvarez fired, but missed. Not by much, Fargo thought as he lay, panting, in a rocky trough, the bullet's whine still ringing in his ears. The next dash, toward the high outcropping, was the longest. Fargo eased his head over the boulder and measured the distance as another bullet whizzed right beside his head. Alvarez was a damn good shot. And he was ready for Fargo to make his last run for it. The odds were good that Alvarez would shoot him. An idea suddenly flashed through Fargo's head.

He spotted an overhang high on the opposite side of the canyon, where the rotten rock was ready to collapse. Fargo gathered his feet under him, then pulled up the Sharps and took aim. He fired once, the shot echoing, but nothing happened. In the next instant, Fargo shifted his aim a bit lower and fired again. This time, the bullet dislodged some of the rock which supported the overhang and the cliff began to crumble. Fargo didn't wait to watch, but dashed out of cover, skittering toward the outcropping, hoping that the bandido would be momentarily distracted by the noise behind him and would turn and look over his shoulder. Fargo was just about to reach cover when the bullet caught him high in the shoulder, tearing through his muscle.

He swore and dove for the rock, coming down hard and rolling behind the boulder. He came up to his feet, rifle in hand, and without pausing, came out from the other side of the outcropping, rifle blazing. He emptied his rifle into the hunched form of Manuel Alvarez, who jumped and twitched and then was still. Fargo waited a long moment, his teeth clenched against the pain in his shoulder. Then he put down his rifle and, pistol in hand, slowly advanced.

The famous bandido lay, face up, his dark eyes open and angry, as his blood pooled beside him, mixing with the blood of the dead horse. It was over.

From the campsite, Fargo heard the occasional pop of gunfire intensify. There seemed to be more shooting. The soldiers were probably making a last assault on the remaining bandits, Fargo thought. He examined his left shoulder. The bullet had passed clean through the muscle of his shoulder. Fargo stripped off his shirt and tore off the sleeves, fashioning a bandage which he tied on tight, using his good arm and his teeth to knot it. If he didn't move too fast, the bleeding would stop soon. He'd see to the wound later. Meanwhile, he'd have to get back to the men.

Fargo hiked across the open canyon toward the bend near the bandidos' campsite. The occasional firing continued. Fargo wondered why the soldiers hadn't managed to kill off the three remaining bandidos in the time since he'd been gone. He moved warily toward the last rock and peered around it. The bodies of the bandidos littered the campsite. Nothing moved. All the bandidos were dead. Every one of them.

The echoes of gunfire were coming from above. Fargo gazed up, his eyes seeking the soldiers. Crouched on the far upper southern lip of the canyon, and firing down at the soldiers crouched halfway down the slope, was a line of dark figures. The soldiers were completely pinned down. The attackers had obviously waited until the soldiers had begun to descend toward the campsite to inspect the dead bandidos, and then sprang an ambush.

Fargo swore, trying to make out the details of the attackers. He spotted a feathered head and braids on another. They were Indians. Crowheart's band. Fargo swore to himself and retreated back through the canyon, reloading as he went. He jammed the rifle through his belt and climbed up the rocks again, pulling himself upward with the powerful muscles of his good arm, until he stood, high over the deep canyon.

Then he inched along the top, keeping rocks between himself and the line of attackers. Finally, they came into view, just fifty yards away, lined up on their bellies, firing downward. There were five of them and they didn't notice him, hidden behind the rock to one side of them, as they devoted their full attention to trying to pick off the men below. They were a nasty bunch, Fargo thought as he looked at them. Some wore buckskins and others were dressed in a motley collection of U.S. Army castoffs. The one lying nearest Fargo wore a belt that sported hanging pieces of dark and light fur—scalps, Fargo knew. Maybe worse.

Fargo raised his Colt slowly. Six bullets for five men. With luck . . .

Fargo fired the first three shots fast, catching the first in the center of the ribs, shifting his aim to the second and plugging him in the back. The third one took a bullet in the side of the head, exploding blood all over the fourth lying next to him. The fourth man rolled in surprise, trying to bring his gun around in an arc toward the sudden attack, but Fargo, shifting the aim up slightly, caught him full in the belly. The fifth managed to get his rifle full around and he squeezed off a shot toward Fargo, which flew wild just as he took a bullet in the neck and spouted like a fountain.

The sixth man hunched instinctively down next to his dead companion, only his gun visible and the top of his head. Fargo took careful aim. It was an impossible shot. An inch off and he'd miss. If the shot was too low, he'd be a dead man. Without a pause, Fargo shifted the aim a hair higher and squeezed the trigger again. An agonized shriek split the air and the Indian raised himself upward, jerking and twitching, his eyes wild, and then collapsed. Fargo waited a moment, but the man didn't move again.

Fargo remained behind cover as he gazed all around at the surrounding rocks and cliffs. Nothing moved. Then he looked down the line of dead men, wondering if one of them was the notorious Crowheart. He remembered seeing drawings of the renegade's broken nose and steely eyes. He poked his head over the cliff and looked down the slope.

"How many men did we lose?" Fargo shouted down.

"So, it's you, Fargo! You ran and hid, you coward!" a voice shouted back. "Let Alvarez escape and left us pinned down here."

Fargo recognized Billy Sullivan's voice. He stepped to the edge of the cliff and spotted Sullivan emerging from behind a rock. Fargo pulled up his rifle and took aim at the soldier's left foot. Then he put the rifle down. All he needed was a lame soldier to haul around.

"Alvarez is dead in the next canyon," Fargo spat back at him and went to inspect the Indians he'd killed.

He turned them over with the toe of his boot. They were a nasty-looking bunch, their faces, even in death, hard and menacing. One had a long ugly red scar down his cheek. None of them was Crowheart. After another long look around him, Fargo quickly descended the slope toward the soldiers.

"How many did we lose?"

"One," Dade said, "and two wounded." Blood ran down the old soldier's face in rivulets. "Just a graze," he said.

The dead soldier, a surly bearded one, had caught one of the Indian's bullets in the back. Another got one through the calf and was moaning. A third sat with his wounded hand wrapped in his shirt. The rest had been bruised and badly grazed from diving rock to rock, but they'd be all right.

Fargo led the way down into the canyon. He kept an eye out over his shoulder, not liking the menacing rocks towering over them. They inspected the bandidos' campsite quickly. Billy Sullivan headed toward the pot of beans beside the fire and began eating them.

"Let's go," Fargo said. They wouldn't stop to bury the bodies. Not with Crowheart and possibly the rest of his band lurking about. "And let's take the horses." The bandidos' horses were saddled and *aparejos* were bunched up on either side, but they didn't stop to look inside them.

Fargo selected a powerful *grullo* and mounted. The gray-blue mount shifted under him, tried to buck him off, then quieted. It had spirit all right, but it was not the Ovaro. Faro worried again about where the black-and-white pinto had gone. He felt almost certain that Crowheart or his band had found and taken the horse. But he had traveled the canyon from one end to the other. Unless they had forced it into one of the narrow, blind side canyons, he would have run into them and his horse.

The soldiers quickly selected horses and tethered the rest into a string. Fargo led the way, back toward where they had left the mules. Fargo realized it had been a mistake to leave the mules with only one guard, and a kid at that. He was blaming himself for his decision as they rounded the corner and came upon the shallow culvert.

Sure enough, the mules were gone. Gone with all their canteens and supplies and extra ammunition. The kid lay sprawled on the ground. Fargo leapt down and saw that the private's neck had been sliced clean through. The artery was still pumping. Dark bloody stumps showed where the boy's ears had been sliced off his head. There was a line across the forehead where the murderer had started to lift the kid's scalp, but had stopped. Crowheart and his butchers couldn't have gotten far.

Fargo stood hastily and remounted, signaling to the men to follow. He led the way up the winding canyon again. At every turn, he felt himself stiffen, expecting to see the retreating Indians as they came around the corner. But each time he was disappointed. He peered at the dark side canyons, but they appeared to be shallow dead ends and it was impossible to find a trail on the bare rocks.

Finally, they came to the slope leading up out of the canyon, where they had first spotted the smoke plume. When they hit the dusty track, Fargo got down off his horse and knelt to inspect the ground.

There were no fresh mule prints leading out of the canyon. Somehow, Crowheart and his band had a secret exit out of Echo Canyon. Fargo glanced up and saw that the sun was lowering.

"Dade, take the men and get into a defensive position over against that short cliff over there. If I don't get back before dark, no fire tonight. And keep your eyes open. Triple guards. Check what's inside the *aparejos* in case there's food and water."

The old sarge nodded.

"I'm going to track our mules," Fargo said. It wasn't really the mules, of course, Fargo added silently. It was the Ovaro. And his own curiosity. Where the hell had they all gone?

"Tracking?" Tommy Gibbons piped up. He squinted up at Fargo and ran his fingers through his red hair until it stood up straight on his head. "My pa used to tell me I could track a bee flying home. Can I come with you, Mr. Fargo?"

Fargo opened his mouth to say no and then thought better of it. The kid was dependable, but green. If he was going to take anybody along, it should be Sergeant Dade. But he needed to leave somebody with some sense in charge and that had to be Dade. Still, if he got in a jam, the kid might prove useful.

"Come along," Fargo said. Tommy mounted the Appaloosa he'd chosen from the bandidos' remuda. Fargo started down the trail with a backward wave to the men gathered around the short cliff. The troublemaker Billy Sullivan was already arguing with Dade about something.

Fargo dismounted the *grullo* when they reached the first narrow canyon, which led off to the right.

"We're going to scour every inch of this canyon," Fargo told Tommy, keeping his voice low. "But while I look at the tracks, I want you to watch our backs. Keep your eyes constantly searching those rocks above us on both sides. If you see anything move, we're taking cover."

Tommy nodded. Fargo's eyes searched the broken rocks, looking for something, anything, out of place. He climbed up into the narrow culvert on foot, but it was blind, as he expected. So was the second one and the third. An hour later, he began to lose hope. They were now only a few hundred yards from the shallow culvert where he'd left the mules and the Ovaro. And the light was leaving the sky above them. The desert air, so blasting hot during the day, was rapidly losing heat. Then he caught it. A whiff of fresh mule dung. Very nearby. He followed his nose and approached a steep wall.

As Fargo drew nearer to the rock wall, he saw that what looked to be solid rock was actually a naturally disguised cleft. Just wide enough for a horse to pass through. Or a bunch of mules. Fargo slipped into the opening and saw, on the rocky path, the fresh mule dung. He signaled Tommy to stay where he was, with his back to the cliff, just at the secret cleft entrance. Fargo went ahead on foot, moving like a silent shadow among the other deepening shadows.

Ten minutes later, Fargo came upon another cleft, at the end of the canyon. He moved like a panther between the rocks, ears alert for the slightest sound. He paused at the edge of the cleft and gazed out, amazed.

Below him was a gentle, barren slope and a wide valley with low hills on the far side. The sun had gone down. The empty sky was pale yellow in the west and darkening behind the stars in the east. Below, the wide land was gathering night. He squinted and tried to pick out any moving figures on the darkening land below. Through a gap between two of the distant hills, he could see the flatlands beyond and he knew that Broken Oak's trading post lay back in that direction. The canyon was a shortcut though the Granite Mountains, bypassing the high trail winding through the peaks. The tracks of the mules and several horses were as plain as writing on the ground before him. Fargo knelt and, in the fading light, examined the tracks closely. In a patch of chalky soil, he saw what he was looking for ... the Ovaro's distinctive large hoofprint among the smaller ones of the mules.

Fargo retraced his steps to where Tommy held the horses. They rode quickly through the shortcut canyon. When they emerged, the sky was fully dark and a cold stiff wind blew out of the west. Fargo considered the options. They could try to track Crowheart and his band in the darkness. How hard could it be to find a string of mules being driven across wide open land?

For a moment, Fargo considered returning to where Dade and the other soldiers were camped. But it would entail several hours' delay. And every hour meant the Ovaro, the mules, and Crowheart were further away. Suddenly, Fargo's shoulder began throbbing in earnest. He'd completely ignored the wound. Now it screamed for his attention. For a moment, he was tempted to stop there, at the entrance of the canyon, to tend to his wound. But he didn't like the place. It was too exposed, there in full view of the wide valley. He signaled Tommy to follow and they descended the barren slope. At the bottom, Fargo saw an arroyo, a deep gash that snaked across the land. He headed toward it and they took shelter beside a cutbank. While Tommy watered the horses, Fargo located half a dozen prickly pear.

"You'll have to help me with this, Tommy," Fargo said. The pain had started up again, the throbbing making the stars dance.

They had to work in the starlight since they didn't dare risk a light of any kind on the wide open land, even in the shelter of the cutbank. At Fargo's instructions, Tommy peeled the cactus pads. Gritting his teeth, Fargo squeezed the juice out of some of them and bathed the wound, using some of his torn shirt to wipe away the blood as the wound opened up again. Tommy swallowed audibly when he saw the blood gushing down Fargo's arm. Fargo told him how to tear up the rest of the shirt to fashion bandages to hold the cactus poultices on, and a sling for his bad arm. Tommy did as he was told, his hands trembling.

As the waves of pain washed over him, Fargo found himself thinking of Katie Conrad back at the trading post. He wondered how she was getting on with her leg wound.

Finally, it was done. Fargo was bare-chested, his

other shirt being in the saddlebag on the Ovaro. Tommy offered his own army shirt, but Fargo refused it. It wouldn't have buttoned across his broad chest anyway. Then he remembered the bandidos' *aparejos*. Tommy pulled the blanket bundles down from the horses and opened them up. There were two canteens of water. Fargo took a long swig and realized how thirsty he'd been. There were a few pieces of beef jerky, a small purse of gold coins, a gold watch and fob, a bowie knife, and a few cans of beans. There was a leather vest, smelly with sweat. Fargo discarded the vest, but wrapped the wool blanket about his shoulders, serape-style. They ate some of the jerky and beans standing up as Fargo looked across the dark land toward the east.

"We're going to walk it, Tommy," Fargo said. "We can't risk stumbling blind into their camp in the middle of the night."

"Tracking on foot," Tommy said enthusiastically. "My pa always said that was the best way."

Fargo led the *grullo* and Tommy led the Appaloosa as they set off. It was a long night. Fargo felt his feet grow heavy and the throbbing in his shoulder sometimes made the star-filled night seem like a distant nightmare. It was an effort to keep his mind on the tracking, to stay alert, ears open to the slightest sound. Several times, they stopped in the middle of the wide open land, listening to the sounds of the night—a startled coyote loping away, or the quiet rustle of scorpions out for their nocturnal ramblings, or twice, the short low call of the burrowing owls. But there was nothing else to be heard. No mules braying, no human voices. No woodsmoke in the air.

It was several hours before dawn when Fargo realized that Crowheart's gang must have decided to drive on through the night. They were almost at the foot of the low hills at the other side of the wide valley. On the other side of the hills lay Broken Oak's Trading Post, although Fargo could not tell exactly where it was. Fargo and Tommy mounted and rode as the dawn crept up slowly in the east.

An hour after dawn, as they rode over the saddle between two hills, they spotted the trading post. Fargo put the *grullo* into a fast gallop as they came down the slope, approaching the post from the backside. They were nearly there, and making a wide circle around the front when Fargo realized something was wrong. Dead wrong.

There were no figures of soldiers marching along the top of the wall. Fargo pulled up his Sharps and motioned for Tommy to do the same. They angled out, well out of rifle range, and came around toward the front of the trading post. One of the wide wooden doors gaped open, hanging on its hinges.

On the other, the figure of a man was stuck on the outside, suspended above the ground in the shape of a cross, his arms out straight. The man's head sagged to one side and he did not stir. A row of brass buttons glittered in the sun. Even from this distance, Fargo recognized Lieutenant Pike. And he saw the dark streaks of blood which stained the wooden door, running down from the man's hands and his head. Lieutenant Pike had been nailed to the wooden door.

5

Fargo pulled up short on the *grullo*. He turned about and his eyes scoured the hills and the bleak empty land stretching to the east in front of the trading post. Nothing moved.

"Jesus, Jesus," Tommy Gibbons muttered as he reined in next to Fargo and sighted the lieutenant, cruelly nailed to the gate of the trading post. The kid was shaky, his face pale. "What about Miss Conrad?" Fargo heard the anger blaze in the Tommy's voice.

"Steady!" Fargo snapped. "Stay here. Keep your eyes open. If you see anything move, fire a warning shot. I'm going inside."

Fargo dismounted and handed the *grullo*'s reins to Tommy. He started forward, his Colt in his good hand. He moved warily, his ears alert for any sound. The wooden gate creaked in the slight breeze. Fargo stopped and glanced up at Pike, whose unseeing eyes were half open, looking down at the ground. His belly had been sliced open and his guts spilled out the front of him. He'd been dead for hours. Fargo peered around the gate into the courtyard.

Inside was chaos. The mauled body of one soldier lay curled on one side in the dirt, blood darkening his crotch and his chest. The fat cook lay belly up, his face a mass of blood and flesh. He was handcuffed to a wagon wheel and he'd been shot at point-blank range. The contents of Broken Oak's house had been strewn all over the yard. What the hell had Crowheart done with Katie and Summer Lightning? And the old trader?

The interior of the little house was dark. Fargo peered inside, expecting the worst. The chairs had been smashed and the pottery shards littered the floor. But there were no more bodies. Fargo felt his relief mixed with red hot fury. The women were still alive. Maybe. But they were in the hands of the worst butcher in the west.

Just then, Fargo heard a shot outside. He whirled about and ran toward the gate. Out beyond the adobe walls, Tommy Gibbons sat on his Appaloosa, his smoking pistol aimed toward the hills.

"Up there!" Tommy shouted excitedly. "I saw somebody!"

Fargo hurried toward Tommy and turned back to see where Tommy was pointing. Sure enough, a small figure was moving against the sere folds of the hills. Moving unsteadily, but plunging down the hillside. Only a moment passed before Fargo recognized Broken Oak. They galloped the horses up the steep hillside toward the old man, who met them halfway.

Broken Oak's face was streaked with blood and he limped badly, a thigh wound darkening his buckskin pants. But his eyes were deadly clear, clear with fury.

"I thought you were dead, Fargo. Crowheart came," he croaked, his voice cracked and dry. "My brother, Crowheart." Fargo dismounted and handed him the canteen of water. The old trader took it gratefully and swigged, then cleared his throat.

"What happened?"

"That lieutenant," Broken Oak said, "dressed down the fat one for not saluting him. Handcuffed him to the wagon. Told the other one to keep watch alone."

"And the man fell asleep," Fargo finished.

"Middle of the night, I heard Miss Katie scream," Broken Oak said. "I was sleeping on the roof. Didn't have my rifle. Stupid. I looked over the top and there were four of them and Crowheart. Already had the gate open and ... dragging ..."

"Summer Lightning and Katie?"

"Didn't stop to do anything to them," Broken Oak said, his voice hard. "Not yet, anyway. They shot the two soldiers and—"

"Yeah, we saw the lieutenant," Fargo cut in.

"Summer Lightning"—his voice broke again and he swallowed hard before going on—"she told Crowheart I had gone to Fort Desoto with some other soldiers to bring the army to help. I think he believed her." Broken Oak's voice was hard as steel. "He is my brother and Summer Lightning's uncle. He knows her. But I do not think blood will make a difference to him. She fought and he pushed her down to the ground. Then one of his men tore her dress. They tied her up and threw her over the horse. She begged him to let her go. He said . . . he said there was white blood in her and she deserved to die for that." Broken Oak shook with helpless fury, his cracked face like stone. "I will kill this brother," Broken Oak continued. "By the Great Spirit who led me here, I will kill my brother Crowheart."

"So, you hid until they left," Fargo said after a moment.

"Yes, yes," Broken Oak said, shaking his head as if to clear it. "They were driving a string of mules and your pinto. When I saw that, I thought Crowheart had killed you."

"Which way did they go?"

"Over the hills. I followed. To save my Summer Lightning. And, to kill him. Just as I reached the top, I saw you riding toward the fort. Another five minutes and I would have missed you."

"We'll get some supplies and then we'll go after them," Fargo said.

They rode back to the fort and gathered up several of the canteens scattered about, refilling them at the pump. The flies were already thick on the gore and the stench was rising in the heat of the morning sun. Inside the house, Fargo found a leather pouch of jerky and another of dried fruit that had been hanging on the wall and overlooked. Broken Oak brought out three extra rifles secreted under a camp bed, along with blankets and a box of extra bullets.

Fargo grabbed a clean shirt from among some of

Broken Oak's scattered things and fashioned a better sling for his bad arm from one of Broken Oak's sheets. The bullet wound in the shoulder was sore as hell. His arm was nearly useless, but there was no time to rest. He refreshed the cactus poultices and they left quickly. There was no time to bury the bodies. The three soldiers would be left to the buzzing flies, the vultures, and the black beetles.

Crowheart had stolen the remaining mules at the trading post, so Broken Oak rode first with Fargo, then with Tommy Gibbons to spell the horses. They rode fast, following the wide swath of mule tracks which cut through the barren hills. Fargo occasionally spotted the Ovaro's tracks mixed in with the other hoofprints. His thoughts whirled around what might be happening to Katie Conrad, traveling with her bad bullet wound, and Summer Lightning. The images of Katie Conrad with her long auburn hair and serious eyes, and the lithe, tanned figure of Summer Lightning rose before him, as did the horrifying picture of Lieutenant Pike nailed to the gate with his guts spilling out. Goddamn Crowheart.

And then there were the men waiting back at the head of Echo Canyon, expecting him to return. They'd probably figured Fargo and Tommy had been caught by Crowheart. But Dade had a good head on his shoulders and the sergeant would probably make the wise decision to wait around a day or two and then march in a retreat back to the trading post.

Just before midday, the tracks angled up a slope to meet with the high trail to Echo Canyon. Fargo realized that Crowheart's band was not heading toward shortcut canyon. Instead, they were taking the winding trail to the top of Echo Canyon. They would run straight into Dade and the soldiers. At this thought, Fargo set his jaw and pushed the *grullo* harder up the trail. The gray-blue horse was foaming at the mouth in the heat, but they pushed on. The Appaloosa, carrying Broken Oak and Tommy, was in a lather, too, but Fargo knew that every minute counted now. He kept his eyes on the land ahead of them.

Fargo doubted that Crowheart knew he was being followed. The renegade assumed his six men had killed all the soldiers in Echo Canyon. He had doubled back to the trading post, driving the mules with him, to finish up the job. And now, he was in retreat, never suspecting that the remaining soldiers were waiting at the top of Echo Canyon and that he had a party on his tail.

The jostling of the horses shot pain through his shoulder with every step. Fargo gritted his teeth. He needed a rest. But later. Much later.

They found the first body a mile from the shallow cliff where Fargo had left the men. The soldier lay facedown, sprawled half under a scraggly mesquite bush. They didn't stop to look, but rode past· and ascended a short rise. Fargo called a halt and they sat for a long moment, listening and looking. Ahead of them, the land lay still and broiling under the midday sun. There was nothing to be heard up ahead—no gunfire, no shouting, no sound of mules. They loaded the extra rifles and rode forward at a slow walk.

"How many men did Crowheart have with him?" Fargo asked.

"Four," Broken Oak said quietly.

As they came around a bend, the second body and a third lay one on top of the other. Fifty yards on, Billy Sullivan, minus his scalp and ears, was spread-eagled across the trail. He had been dead only a matter of minutes, Fargo could see. But where was Dade? Fargo began to hope against hope that the old sarge had somehow survived the attack. They did not speak as they slowly ventured forward, ears alert.

Still Fargo heard and saw nothing ahead as they reached the top of the trail, which plunged into Echo Canyon. The shallow cliff where he had left the men was deserted. They sat for several minutes under the broiling sun, listening, waiting. Then Fargo heard a soft rustle. He rolled off his mount and crouched beside the horse, his rifle at the ready. Behind him, Broken Oak and Tommy slid down.

Fargo waited expectantly, then heard a low moan from behind some nearby rocks. A trap? Fargo surveyed the slopes around them, but nothing moved.

"Cover me," he said. He dashed forward, Colt in hand, and vaulted over the rocks, almost landing on the man who lay there. It was the sarge, bloodied and barely conscious. Fargo called for Tommy to bring him a canteen while Broken Oak kept watch. Fargo holstered his pistol and pulled Dade half upright and the old soldier's eyes fluttered as he tried to open them.

"Fargo!" Dade mumbled. His eyes rolled back

again and he sagged. He had a helluva goose egg on the side of his head, but Fargo couldn't see any bullet wounds. Fargo dashed some of the water on his face and his eyes opened again. Fargo gave him a drink and Dade's lips moved slowly. "Billy Sullivan. He got the men all stirred up. Said you'd never come back. Deserted. They've all deserted, I guess. Wanted me to go, too, and had to fight 'em."

Dade rubbed his face slowly with his hand, shaking his head to clear it.

"They're all dead," Fargo said. "Crowheart caught them a mile up the trail. Killed them and took the horses. If you hadn't been knocked out behind this rock, he'd have got you, too."

Dade blinked, trying to take in the news. He got to his feet shakily and Fargo held out an arm to steady him. The old sarge glanced up and spotted Broken Oak with the two horses. He looked quizzically at Fargo.

"Crowheart hit the trading post. . . ."

"Miss Conrad?"

"And Summer Lightning. Took 'em both."

"Let's get going," Dade said. He took a step forward, but stumbled.

"Take it easy," said Fargo. There was no time to lose.

Dade and Broken Oak sat on the two horses. Fargo and Tommy walked ahead as they started down the trail into Echo Canyon. As the high rocks rose about them, Fargo felt hesitation prick him and he stopped. Tommy stopped, too.

The damned canyon where they'd ambushed Manuel Alvarez could just as likely be their own deathtrap, Fargo thought. And another possibility struck him suddenly. Crowheart had left his six men firing down at the soldiers who were ambushing Manuel Alvarez. He'd ridden away assuming his men would finish them off. But the six bodies of his men now lay on the rocks, along with the dead bandidos. When Crowheart reached them, he'd know that some of the soldiers were still around. And maybe hunting him. Then he'd become twice as wary and begin watching his back.

Damn. His instinct screamed at him not to plunge into Echo Canyon. And he listened to it. He cast his mind back to when he had stood in Colonel Power's office, looking at the map with the wide, blank spaces and the sinuous line of Rio Chingo snaking across the empty land up to the lonely fort. He remembered seeing the humps of the Granite Mountains which angled away to the northwest. There had to be another way over them.

"We're going back," Fargo said. Broken Oak opened his mouth to protest, but Fargo cut him short. "It's the only way to save them. We'll double back and rescue them. But for now, we have to make Crowheart think we've given up."

Fargo walked around several times, leaving clear bootprints in the dust, then turned the horses about and led them back up the slope. Once they gained the rise, he and Tommy mounted and they rode the horses, each with two riders, back in the direction of the trading post, through the hills. The horses, laboring under the weight of two men each, were taking it hard. Fargo had just begun to doubt his decision when he saw what he was looking for just ahead—a long swath of molten rock bordering the trail and climbing up an exposed hillside. The trail became rocky and Fargo, with Dade sitting behind him, brought the *grullo* up onto the solid rock and was followed by the Appaloosa bearing Tommy and Broken Oak.

They dismounted immediately to give the horses a rest and hiked quickly over the sizzling solid rock toward a slope of scree. They led the horses toward a rocky culvert leading down the other side of the hill. Fargo instructed the others to go ahead. He hunched down in the shade between two boulders and waited. He changed the bandages on his wound, glad to see the hole was closing quickly with tenderness but no red streaks, no sign of major infection. He drank a little of the warm water in his canteen, then chewed on some jerky and dried berries as his eyes continually roved the wide land spread below him.

An hour passed before he saw movement. And then suddenly, there they were, two figures on horseback winding slowly up the distant trail, eyes on the ground. Fargo immediately scanned the horses, but neither was his Ovaro. The two Indians came on, intently following the trail. Fargo held his breath as they neared the place where he had led them off the trail and onto the molten rockfield. But ten yards before they reached the spot, suddenly one held up his hand and they halted. Fargo knew he was looking at Crowheart.

Even from this distance, Fargo could tell Crowheart was tall and muscular. The Indian sat tall on his horse, wearing a black hat with one long feather and red shirt. Crowheart looking steadily ahead for a long moment. Fargo held his breath as he silently commanded the renegade to give up the search. He watched as Crowheart slowly lowered himself into his saddle and then turned his horse back around toward Echo Canyon.

Fargo waited until the two figures disappeared before he breathed a sigh of relief. Crowheart had believed what he wanted him to believe, that a couple of straggling soldiers had found the four dead bodies and had given up the chase and gone for more help. And with six of his own men dead, Crowheart would be less likely to pursue. If he believed they had really retreated, he'd be off his guard. Maybe.

After they disappeared in the direction of Echo Canyon, Fargo waited another hour, but the land below him remained still in the afternoon heat. The exhaustion of riding through two whole days and a night without sleep began to settle heavily on Fargo. He got to his feet and followed the others.

Just after dusk, he found them, holed up in a shallow cave in a box canyon choked with sagebrush. Tommy was already asleep, rolled up in a blanket. The campsite was easily defensible and a cool spring bubbled out of the canyon wall nearby, running for a short distance before disappearing between the rock crevices at the bottom of the canyon. They refilled the canteens, watered the horses well, and bathed. They didn't risk a fire and took turns standing guard throughout the night. Fargo, wrapped in a blanket, slept fitfully, his dreams crowded with soldiers nailed to doors and Crowheart riding Katie Conrad like a horse.

Fargo awoke well before dawn and refreshed himself at the cold spring. He unwrapped the bandages from his shoulder and let the arm hang free. It hurt bad, but the wound was closed. He'd take off the sling and try to use it a little and work the stiffness out of it. The muscle would take a long time to knit, but meanwhile, he could use the arm a little.

In the darkness of predawn, he watered the horses again, then woke the others. They hit the trail within minutes. Again, Fargo and Tommy led while Broken Oak and Dade rode the horses. Dade offered to walk, but Fargo knew the old soldier hadn't recovered from his concussion yet.

They traveled all day, circling the feet of the high mountains, zigzagging across the slopes to climb up and over the saddles between the hills. By the time the sun was lowering in the west, Fargo calculated they'd traveled only about fifteen miles as far as the crow flew, but at least twice that distance in winding back and forth through the hills. At some point, they should have come out of the Granite Mountains to look down at the nameless dry lake bed at the mouth of Rio Chingo.

The purple shadows were long on the hills and Fargo was just beginning to think he'd miscalculated when they came to the crest of a hill and found themselves looking down at the blood red sunset and a huge alkali flat below them. As they watched, the sun slipped below the sharp horizon.

Fargo stood in the dying light, memorizing the

landscape below him, the way the rocky culvert poured down the hillside at his feet, forming a perfect campsite. He thought he caught a ruby glint of water among the rocks. The culvert connected with a web of shallow arroyos which sliced the braided dusty flats. He imprinted into his mind the distance and the color of the soil where the lakebed fed into the wide mouth of Rio Chingo, a wide dry riverbed that led northward, like a gigantic dusty coiling road. There was no cover on the wide flat. Once you ventured out onto it, there was no place to hide once the Granite Mountains petered out.

A distant movement caught Fargo's eye, far to the left, at the base of the hills on which they stood. He signaled the others and they retreated silently, swiftly, pulling the horses back over the top of the hill. Then Fargo told them to remain under cover and, taking his Sharps, he crept forward again on elbows and belly, slowly, slowly, until he lay beneath a scraggly sage. He pulled the branches apart gently until he had a clear view.

Far below in the dusk, Fargo's sharp eyes spotted the four renegade Indians. They rode, spread out in a diamond, driving the mules and horses between them. Crowheart in his feathered hat rode far to the front. At the center of the herd was the Ovaro, a hunched and blanketed figure on its back—Katie Conrad, Fargo figured. Summer Lightning rode alongside her. As he watched, he thought he could see Summer Lightning gazing up at the slopes, searchingly. He longed to signal to her, but he knew if he did the renegades would spot him, too.

Suddenly, Summer Lightning spurred her horse, which cut through the jostling mules and headed toward the mountain slope. She made a curious motion with her arms and Fargo realized she had freed her hands, which had been bound. He guessed she'd been working them free for hours. He watched helplessly as the renegades shouted to one another. Damn, they were well out of rifle range. He considered moving down the slope to get in closer, but realized they'd spot him well before he could do any good with his Sharps. Fargo's grip tightened on his rifle, but there was nothing he could do. A useless gunshot would betray their presence and their only advantage now was surprise.

Summer Lightning's escape attempt was futile, Fargo saw. Crowheart came about at once on his horse and streaked toward Summer Lightning on a diagonal as she headed toward the base of the mountain. One of the other renegades galloped after her in hot pursuit. Her horse was not a fast one. Fargo watched as the two Indians slowly closed in on her like pincers.

As he came within range of her, Crowheart drew his rifle and, holding it by the barrel, swung it toward her. She ducked and the butt glanced off her shoulder and he swung it again, knocking her off her horse. Summer Lightning hit the ground and rolled over once. Fargo felt his blood boil as he watched her bravely come to her feet and continue running toward the mountain. Crowheart whooped in glee and came about again, swinging the rifle. This time it caught her in the back of the head.

Even at this distance, Fargo could see that the blow, hard against the skull, had been fatal. Summer Lightning slumped to the ground and did not move again. Crowheart pulled up cruelly on his horse and dismounted, approaching the inert woman. He kicked her body angrily. Then he slowly drew his knife.

Fargo did not wait to see more. There was nothing he could do now. Summer Lightning was dead. He slowly eased himself back over the hill to where the others waited, thankful that Broken Oak had not witnessed the scene. He said nothing about Summer Lightning.

"We stay here for now," Fargo said. "They'll camp in the culvert at the bottom of the hill. When it's dark, we go in."

It was better that Broken Oak not know what had happened to his daughter, Fargo decided. Not now. Not yet. A man maddened by rage made mistakes. And there could be no mistakes.

6

They rested for two hours over the crest of the hill, with Tommy Gibbons keeping watch on the Indians. Just as Fargo had expected, the renegades had camped in a shallow rocky depression near the spring, at the base of the rockslide-choked culvert which poured down the hillside. He was surprised to see that the Indians lit a campfire.

"Crowheart must have really let down his guard," Fargo said thoughtfully when he returned from surveying the campsite, bringing Tommy with him. "Now, here's my plan. Broken Oak and I will climb down through the culvert using the rock as cover. Dade, you take Tommy and hike south until you're well away from the camp. Then come down the front of the slopes and double back, creeping up that arroyo."

"We'll hit them from two sides at once," said Dade. "But they're sure to have guards."

"There'll be one guard out at the edge of the arroyo," Fargo said. "You get him, just keep it quiet. We'll take care of the one by the mules. Then, when I fire the first shot, at about midnight, we'll rush the camp."

Fargo went to the two horses and took the two saddle blankets. The thick wool was redolent with the sweat of the horses. He pulled the blade from his ankle holster and made a long slit in the center of each blanket. He slid one over his head like a short poncho and handed the other to Broken Oak.

"Wear this," Fargo said. "Then we'll smell like a horse when we get in there among the mules."

Broken Oak nodded and slipped it on. They started down the culvert, painstakingly lowering themselves, inch by inch, careful not to dislodge any rocks, moving like shadows from one boulder to the next under the pale starlight. The dying campfire below flickered enticingly, but did not throw off much light. Fargo could hardly see; the figures gathered around it were just dark, moving shapes.

They had been crawling down the rocks for more than an hour and were only a hundred yards above the camp when Broken Oak stumbled and a stone clattered down the hillside, the cracking sound of rock on rock carrying for a long way. Fargo shrank back into the shadows, as did the old trader. Fargo's sharp eyes picked out the form of one of the Indians as he leapt to his feet, his rifle ready. Broken Oak cursed in a whisper. Fargo could feel the tension in the air—all the renegades below would now be on guard. Still, he could only make out one of the Indians standing next to the fire, his rifle across his chest, looking up toward the rocky culvert.

But luck was with them. Just then, a coyote howled nearby on the hillside and the renegade standing below raised his rifle at the sound and fired a shot. The coyote yelped agonized and spun off through the brush. They were close enough now to the campsite that they heard the renegade laugh cruelly. Then the dark figure melted back into the shadows around the fire, which had died down to red embers.

The Indian below was a dead sure shot, Fargo thought. He had plugged the coyote on the hillside from the sound only. Fargo and Broken Oak waited ten minutes before daring to move again. After a time, they inched forward again until they had nearly reached the dark, shifting mass of hobbled mules and horses.

Moving as slowly as floating ducks, they drifted in among the sleeping animals on the far side of the remuda. Fargo and Broken Oak, hunched down, hid among the humped backs of the stock. The stink of the saddle blankets they wore masked their human odor and none of the mules or horses were alarmed. The animals stirred slightly, like water under a breeze, as they eased through. Fargo kept his eyes open for the guard. They came closer to the campfire and still he had not seen a guard on the livestock. It didn't make sense.

Just ahead, among the animals, Fargo caught a glimpse of the white-and-black markings of his Ovaro. He edged his way toward the magnificent pinto. It raised its head and bent its neck to look at him as he came up. Fargo hoped it wouldn't nicker. It somehow seemed to understand the need for silence and gently nuzzled him. Fargo ran his hand along the horse's side, feeling its lean ribs. It had been running hard and had not been well fed, but a few weeks of rest would put it right. He bent down and pulled the blade from his ankle holster, then sliced the rawhide hobble from its legs. He patted its nose so it would remain among the mules for the time being. Then he and Broken Oak moved on until they stood at the edge of the animals, looking out at the camp.

There were two figures rolled up in blankets beside the fire, which gave off only a ruddy glow. Fargo swore to himself. He looked closely and spotted a tangle of auburn hair emerging from one of the bedrolls. That one was Katie Conrad and the other was an Indian.

His trigger finger twitched as he thought of the possibility that it was Crowheart himself lying in the bedroll. But that still left four more of the renegades, maybe including Crowheart, somewhere out in the dark. Fargo felt the hair on the back of his neck prickle. He didn't like it one bit. Where the hell was the guard on the livestock? And where were the others?

In the dim light, Broken Oak looked at him quizzically. He pointed at the two sleeping figures and then carved woman figures in the air. Broken Oak assumed the two sleepers were Katie and Summer Lightning, Fargo realized. He signaled Broken Oak to keep them covered.

By now, Dade and Tommy Gibbons were out by the arroyo. Since he had heard nothing, they had either managed to kill the guard without making a sound, or else they had found nothing. Fifteen minutes passed as Fargo waited, hoping to spot someone changing guards or something. But nothing moved.

He tried to figure out what Crowheart might have had in mind. Was it possible he and his men were sleeping some distance away from the fire, just in case of an attack like this one? If so, it was devilishly clever. Fargo realized there was only one way to find out and that was to scout out the area. He signaled to Broken Oak to remain among the mules and he silently slipped back through them, and then began a slow circle, moving like a cloud across the night landscape.

For another full hour, he quietly worked his way around the campsite, finding nothing. Finally, he came out toward where the arroyo sliced the flatland. He spotted a humped shape in the starlight and knelt to inspect the body—a renegade with his throat sliced.

Just then, Fargo was seized from behind and he felt thick hands around his neck and the cool metal of a blade against his throat. He reached around and grasped the man's hair.

"It's me, Fargo," he gagged, trying to keep quiet. The strong arms holding him released him instantly. Fargo whirled about and pulled Dade down to the ground with him. They knelt silently for ten minutes while they listened to the silence of the night. Finally, Fargo relaxed.

"We killed one guard. I thought you were another," Dade whispered.

"There's only one renegade by the campfire with Katie," Fargo said. "I came looking for the others, but they're not around."

"Tommy's right over there. We scoured the arroyos," Dade said. "If they were there, they're gone now."

"I don't like it," Fargo said. "But we'll have to go in."

It was getting late. Dawn was only a few hours away. If they were going to strike, it would have to be soon. Fargo considered for another moment. One guard dead. One asleep by the fire. Three more missing, maybe including Crowheart.

"You and Tommy spread out," Fargo said. "Keep your eyes open. Broken Oak and I will get the one at the fire. Whatever happens, don't come into the fire. Stay out here. Then we'll see what else turns up."

In another fifteen minutes, Fargo stood beside a rock, looking down into the camp at the two motionless figures and Katie's auburn hair in a red-glinting cascade, spread upon the ground. There was something fishy about the whole thing. The dark figure of Broken Oak stood almost invisible among the mules, waiting. Fargo signaled him to bring up his rifle and give him cover.

Soundlessly, Fargo drew his Colt. He lifted it slowly and took aim at the blanketed form without the auburn hair. He started to squeeze the trigger and then, at the last instant, his instinct told him something was wrong. His finger loosened and, still holding the Colt before him, he advanced on the sleepers until he stood over them. Broken Oak stepped out of the shadows, his rifle ready.

Inside the blankets, both of the sleepers awakened. Fargo could tell by the sudden small jerks as they came to consciousness and then lay there, still wrapped in the blankets, with stiffened bodies.

Suddenly, Fargo kicked the blanket away from the form with the auburn hair. In an instant, Fargo knew he'd guessed right as his eyes took in the hanks of Katie's cut hair bound by a piece of rope. In a flash, the wiry Indian lying on the blanket rolled over and brought up his rifle.

With another swift kick, Fargo dislodged the bar-rel as the gun roared, the bullet flying wide. Without a pause and forgetting his bad shoulder, Fargo threw himself down on the man, grappling for his hands. The Indian was small, but strong as sinew. They rolled over and over as they struggled, nearing the fire. Fargo rolled on top of the Indian, his powerful right arm pinning the renegade under him.

His left arm exploded with pain as the Indian lunged upward with one fist. They were just inches from the fire and Fargo felt the hair on his beard curl in the heat and could smell his hair burning as they struggled. The Indian spat in his face and suddenly brought up his knee. Fargo felt an explosion of pain in his groin and loosened his grip for an instant. Broken Oak came running up, trying to get a clear shot.

"Cover that one," Fargo shouted. Broken Oak pointed his rifle at the other blanketed figure, who had not stirred.

The renegade wrenched one arm loose and reached toward the fire, grasping a stick with a red burning coal tip. He jammed it upward into Fargo's chest, where it sizzled and burned. Fargo clenched his jaw and brought his bad arm around, dislodging the burning stick and forcing it downward until it rested against the renegade's cheek. The Indian screamed in agony as the coal slowly sizzled against his flesh.

"Where's Crowheart?" Fargo asked.

The renegade's eyes flashed pure hatred. Fargo asked the question again in Algonquian and repeated it in an Athapascan dialect the Apache used. The man moaned in agony and finally spoke.

"Gone. Gone."

"Where?"

For a moment, the Indian remained silent. Fargo removed the burning brand.

"There are forty soldiers surrounding this camp," Fargo lied. "We killed your friend out by the arroyo. Now talk."

"Crowheart is going north. We rendezvous with him in two days' time. At Fort Chingo."

Fargo's eyes narrowed.

"Why Fort Chingo?"

"There is a white man there ..." the renegade said. Just then, Fargo's attention was distracted for an instant by Broken Oak, who had begun to poke the other blanketed figure with his rifle barrel.

"Where is Summer Lightning?" Broken Oak asked distractedly, as if talking to the other person in the blankets.

Suddenly, the Indian he was holding down seemed to explode upward with all his force, jamming his fist upward into Fargo's bad shoulder. The pain knocked Fargo straight back and the Indian slipped out from beneath him and rolled to his feet, grabbing Fargo's Colt and kicking his rifle well out of reach. Fargo slowly got to his feet, his hands raised, cursing inwardly.

"Drop that gun," the renegade said to Broken Oak. The old trader hesitated a moment and the renegade pulled the trigger. The shot kicked up a fan of dirt beside Broken Oak's foot. He leapt aside and threw down the rifle with a curse.

"Forty soldiers?" laughed the renegade. He retreated a few steps, circling the fire, his eyes never leaving them and keeping his back toward the mules and horses. Fargo swore silently. Goddamn it, he'd told Dade to stay out by the arroyo no matter what. And Dade was such a good soldier, he'd do what he was told. For once, obeying orders was the wrong thing.

"I don't think there are any soldiers," the Indian jeered. "White men lie. I think Crowheart will reward me when I bring the scalps of two more white men to him. You are first."

The Indian raised the rifle and aimed at Broken Oak's chest. Fargo whistled. The renegade sneered, just as a flurry of motion erupted behind him. The Indian, caught off guard, whirled about and was struck full out as the Ovaro plunged forward. The Indian was knocked off his feet and fell onto the red hot coals, belly first. He shrieked in agony. The Ovaro veered off to one side. Fargo seized the rifle and shot the Indian dead, then dragged the body out of the coals.

The pinto shifted nervously at the smell of burned flesh. The mules brayed. Fargo turned his attention to the other figure in the blanket. He knelt on the ground and put one hand out to touch the blanketed form.

"Katie?" he said. "It's me, Skye Fargo." He was dead sure it was Katie Conrad in the blanket. He had been able to tell when he was standing over them, by the size and shapes of the bodies, who was lying where, despite the switch of auburn hair. "You're all right, Katie."

He heard a muffled whimper and he slowly pulled back the blanket. She lay, curled up, her blue eyes large and frightened. Her hair had been chopped off her head and she looked like a boy. When she saw his face, she flinched.

Fargo pulled her up toward him and she came, reluctant at first, as if disbelieving. He put his arms around her, holding her close.

"It's all right," he murmured. "You are safe now." She clung to him as if afraid to ever let him go.

"But where is Summer Lightning?" Broken Oak muttered. Fargo felt Katie stiffen at the words. He started to stand, but she wouldn't let go of him. Fargo picked her up in his arms and got to his feet. Pain roared down his left shoulder but he ignored it.

"Follow me," Fargo said to Broken Oak. First he walked out toward the arroyos where he had left Dade and Tommy. When he arrived at the spot, there was no one there. Then Dade materialized beside him, rising out of a shallow gully. He left Katie Conrad with Dade and Tommy and led the old trader across the gulch-carved land he'd memorized from above toward the spot where he'd seen

Crowheart kill Summer Lightning that afternoon. The night was silent as a sliver of new moon rose above the peaks. Fargo was just starting to think they had missed the spot when he saw a dark form lying on the flat before them.

"Crowheart killed her this afternoon," Fargo said. "I'm sorry."

The old trader limped toward the body and turned her face upward. Fargo, standing a short distance away could see, even in the dim light, that her breasts and genitals had been mutilated. Broken Oak threw back his head and howled, a cry of sorrow and rage so profound that for a moment Fargo imagined that however far away the bastard Crowheart might be, he would surely hear it.

Broken Oak bent over and gathered Summer Lightning into his arms. He could barely straighten up, but when Fargo stepped forward to help him, the old man shook his head. Fargo headed back toward the camp and Broken Oak followed for a short way, struggling to carry Summer Lightning.

When Fargo glanced back, he saw that the old man had angled off toward the hills. Fargo knew Broken Oak would chant and pray over his daughter and would build a rock cairn over her body. He also knew that because Summer Lightning's body had been mutilated, she could not go to the happy hunting ground in the next life. Instead, as the Indians believed, she would wander as a homeless unhappy spirit for eternity. And Broken Oak, if it was the last thing he did on earth, would avenge his daughter's death.

By the time Fargo returned to the camp, he had

made up his mind they would not rest there. There was a slight possibility Crowheart might return to the site. But, more than that, the smell of death clung to the place. Fargo brought Katie back to the campsite and helped her onto the Ovaro. Then he mounted behind her.

"Bring a couple of the best horses," Fargo said, "and follow me up the hill. We'll sleep on top tonight and keep watch from above. Leave the mules near the spring. It will save us trouble watering them in the morning."

By the time they reached the summit, it was almost dawn. Dade volunteered for the first watch. Tommy rolled himself into a blanket beside their horses. Fargo found a rock overhang which would provide a nice piece of shade as the sun rose. He spread some blankets out and suggested Katie try to get some rest. He changed the bandages on her leg wound, which was red and tender, but healing. Then he lay down beside her.

"Please don't leave me, Skye," she said, nestling close to him. He stroked her shorn head and saw her eyes fill with memories of the last two days. "I was sure I was going to die. I prayed to die, quickly. Like Summer Lightning. When I woke up by the campfire and heard your voice, I thought I was dreaming. I didn't want to wake up."

Suddenly she was sobbing, letting out all of the fear and pain of her captivity. Fargo held her close for a long time and finally, she wiped her face against his shirt. Then she took his hand and guided it to her soft, pillowy breast. She smiled at him.

"Please. Hold me," Katie whispered, her words full of need. "Tell me I'm really alive again."

Fargo gathered her against him as though his powerful arms could keep away all that had terrified her.

"You're alive, Katie Conrad," he whispered into her hair later as she lay dozing in the shade, curled beside him. His thoughts turned to Crowheart then and he could not sleep. The words of the renegade he'd fought came back to him. A white man alive at Fort Chingo. Maybe it was Major Conrad. Fargo shook his head, disbelieving. After all these years. Alive. Maybe Katie had been right all along.

A dry scuttling noise awoke Fargo and he opened his eyes slowly. The noonday sun beat down beyond the line of shade where he lay with Katie. Dade and Tommy Gibbons sat side by side on the rocks not far away. Fargo's boots lay overturned near his feet. Fargo heard the sound again. He sat up and grabbed his boots and turned them over. Three large scorpions dropped out and sped away, their stinging tails curved up over their heads. They disappeared into rock crevices. This was scorpion country, Fargo thought as he stood and pulled on his boots. The devils, which hid from the sun during the day and hunted at night, could give you a nasty bite. One bite wasn't fatal, but twenty or more would be.

"Anything moving?" Fargo asked as he joined Dade and Tommy.

"Quiet as a tomb," Dade said, his eyes squinting against the light. "What do we do now?"

"Fort Chingo," Fargo said. It was only ten miles up the winding Rio Chingo. "That Indian last night told me they were set to meet Crowheart in two days' time at the fort. There's a white man there."

Dade started in surprise and glanced at Katie's sleeping form.

"Does she know?"

"She was lying by the fire when he said it," Fargo said. "But I'm not sure. In any case, it doesn't matter. She's convinced her father is alive."

"Crowheart still has two men with him," Fargo calculated. "And, unless I'm mistaken, he doesn't know we're on his tail."

"So what's the plan?" Dade asked.

Fargo stared thoughtfully toward the mouth of Rio Chingo, barren and open as a road to hell.

"I don't know," he answered. "It depends on what we find at the fort."

They rode up Rio Chingo bunched up close. All except for Broken Oak, who had appeared just as they were preparing to leave the campsite. The old man's eyes were empty of all but hatred and he didn't speak a word. When they set off, Broken Oak rode far to the rear in the dust, driving the mules.

The riverbed, a flat expanse of hard-packed sand, wound back and forth between two low cutbanks. There were no rocks and few shrubs. Just cracked earth and heat and dust. They made good time, galloping most of the way to the fort. Despite the danger and uncertainty of what lay ahead, Fargo gloried in the feel of the Ovaro beneath him again.

The sturdy pinto responded to his every motion and he knew its gaits, its limits, and its strengths from all the years together on the trail.

They were a mile out from Fort Chingo when Fargo halted. He had spotted something ahead, something that did not belong to the tawny landscape, something white and tall. Moving. He rode ahead slowly until his eyes made sense of what he saw in the distance.

In the center of the dry riverbed was planted a stick. On top of it, nodding slightly in the relentless wind, was a human skull. The empty eyes stared at them as they rode past, the jawbone still half attached but slack as though in a silent scream. Fargo, riding alongside Katie, noticed that she shuddered but forced herself to look at it before turning away.

As the riverbed narrowed, they came upon another skull and another, as they rode. Soon, the grinning masks were everywhere, in the riverbed and planted on the sides of the cutbanks, a silent regiment of the dead. Ahead, Fargo spotted the solitary shape of Fort Chingo, a desolate hump of adobe on a sizzling flat of alkali.

Just as he had imagined, the gate of the fort gaped open. And nothing moved. Fargo called a halt.

"I'm going in," he said, drawing the Colt with a whisper. "Cover me."

He rode forward on the Ovaro and noticed that Broken Oak had pulled up from behind the mules and followed him as well, a silent shadow. The Ovaro's nostrils flared, but the horse did not stutter or whinny. They clopped on, slowly, through the wide gate and into the deserted yard. All was still. Fargo glanced around at the dusty and broken-down army wagons and the smashed barrels and the blank windows of the low barracks which lined one interior wall.

In the center of the yard was a round hole, eight feet across. Fargo wondered what it was. Some kind of well, maybe? He dismounted and slowly approached, ears alert to any sound around them.

The hole was deep and he had to stand at the edge to see down to the bottom, twenty feet below. The pit was filled with bones. Human bones. And on top of them was something wrapped in a blanket.

Suddenly, the blanket moved. Fargo tightened his finger on the trigger. A corner of the blanket lifted and a head emerged, the face hidden by the filthy lanks of long gray hair.

A hand pushed away the hair and a face looked up at him, the deep-set eyes blank. The man's voice, when he spoke, was a croak.

"Have you brought me another blanket? For my wife?"

Fargo knew he was looking at all that remained of Major William Conrad. The major was stark, raving mad.

7

"William Conrad," Fargo said, hoping that calling the man by name might penetrate his insanity. "You're Major Conrad."

The long-haired scarecrow winced and looked up at Fargo quizzically. Broken Oak joined Fargo on the lip of the pit and gazed down.

"I brought your daughter," Fargo said. "I brought Katie here with me."

The reaction was immediate. Conrad stomped on the bones beneath his feet. Fargo saw a host of scorpions emerge from the bones. Several of them crawled up the major's leg beneath his ragged pants. Suddenly, Fargo realized the pit was swarming with scorpions, on the walls, and crawling over the blanket. Broken Oak came up behind him.

"No! No! She cannot come here! No!" the major rasped.

"Shit," Fargo said. "Look at those scorpions. Why the hell isn't he dead?"

Broken Oak peered down at the crazed man, who continued to stomp on the bones.

"An old Indian trick," the old trader said thoughtfully. "Pinching off the stinger. Medicine men sometimes did it to impress strangers. Make themselves look invulnerable."

At Broken Oak's words, Fargo saw that the scorpions on the major's leg were lashing at him with their tails, but there were no pincers.

"But why?" Fargo asked.

Major Conrad looked up suddenly, as if the question were addressed to him.

"The horror. To torture me," he said suddenly, his eyes suddenly clear. "To keep me company. To make me think I am losing my mind." A wave of confusion swept over his face again, mingled with fear. "He is coming again. He always comes and brings me food and water. I am out of water." He gestured to a pair of canteens hanging on the wall of the pit. "That means he will be coming soon."

"Let's get him out of there before Katie sees him," Fargo muttered. He looked about and spotted a length of rope hanging on one of the broken wagons. They lowered it to the major but couldn't talk him into climbing out. Finally, Fargo tied one end of the rope to the wagon and lowered himself into the stinking pit. As his foot touched the bones in the bottom, his boot and pants leg were instantly crawling with scorpions. He tied the rope around the major's waist and they hauled the man up out of the pit. Then Broken Oak lowered the rope again and Fargo climbed out quickly. The major was cowering beside the pit, covering his head with his arms.

Fargo quickly inspected the rest of the fort and found it deserted. Then he walked to the gate and signaled for the others to come inside. Katie galloped forward, followed by Dade and Tommy driving the mules. When she reached the gate and spotted the figure of her father, she cried out and dismounted. She ran toward him and knelt down beside him. At the touch of her hand, the major jumped away, his face fearful.

"No, Katie! No! You must not come here! He will wrap you in a blanket." The man sobbed. "A blanket. You will die, too."

Katie Conrad put her arms around the man and hugged him close, despite the stench and the filth. Fargo shook his head and spoke his confusion out loud.

"A blanket? What is that about? He mentioned blankets in his letters to Katie."

Broken Oak, standing beside him, looked up.

"It is Crowheart's revenge," he said quietly. "Years ago, when the major was in Kansas Territory, there was a smallpox epidemic. Afterward, the army was ordered to distribute the blankets that the sick had used. They gave them to my tribe and to others. They did this on purpose and many died. Crowheart was the only one to understand the blankets, among all my people."

Broken Oak's eyes were distant with painful memories.

"Was that on Major Conrad's orders?"

"No," Broken Oak said. "The major was fair to the tribes, even though he was a strong enemy when he had to fight. But Crowheart blamed him anyway and he swore to avenge the death of our people. He took the Indian blankets from our dead and dressed himself as a trader. The major's wife bought a blanket from him and she died. The major never forgot. He tried to find Crowheart for years after. Each of them hated the other. Each of them was full of hate. They are both crazy."

"And Conrad followed Crowheart all the way down here," Fargo said. "That explains why he wouldn't return to Fort Desoto when the colonel ordered him to."

"My brother Crowheart comes here tomorrow," Broken Oak said. "That is when I will kill him."

"We will all kill him," said Fargo. "And the two men with him."

Fargo spent the afternoon readying them all for battle. They cleaned and reloaded all the firearms. First he inspected every corner of the fort. He was amazed to find stores of ammunition in the barracks room—barrels of gunpowder, bars of lead, and bullet molds. There were marks on the floor where other barrels and crates had stood and Fargo guessed that Crowheart and his band had been hauling it away little by little. Then he checked every inch of the perimeter wall for breaches in case they were in for a long siege. There were none. He stood on the lookout at the front of the fort, ducked low and looking out. The empty land around the fort seemed to peer in at them, menacing. Crowheart was out there somewhere. And Fargo didn't want the wily renegade to spot him prancing about on top of the fort. Not before he came inside the adobe walls.

He appointed Tommy Gibbons to take care of the livestock and to hobble them just outside the fort. When Crowheart arrived, he would assume his own men were inside. He set the old sarge to watch duty. Katie and her father sat in the dappled shade under an overhang of ocatilla. The major, washed and with his long hair tied back, already looked better, but his mind wandered and he babbled at times like a child. He sat quietly beside his daughter, playing absently with a piece of string. Broken Oak followed Fargo around the fort as he planned the ambush.

Tommy would hide in one of the wagons, his rifle aimed between the slats. Katie and her father would stay inside the adobe barracks room, out of the line of fire. Broken Oak and Dade would be positioned behind a row of barrels. Fargo would keep watch from on top of the wall. The problem was that once they came inside, Fargo would be fully visible standing on the lookout. So he planned to wait until they headed in, then slip down from the wall to secret himself behind the half-open gate.

By evening, all was ready. The Indian had said Crowheart would come in two days' time, which meant tomorrow. Still, Fargo did not want to take the chance in case the Indian showed up early. As night fell they ate a quick meal in silence and took turns sleeping and keeping watch. Fargo was asleep when he felt a hand on his shoulder and he woke up. Broken Oak stood there, ready to be relieved. Fargo got up quickly, strapped on his Colt, took up his Sharps, and climbed to the top of the wall. Dawn was still two hours off and the desert air blew chill. Broken Oak poked about in the wagon for a while and came up with a pair of leather gloves. Then he slung a blanket across his shoulder and began walking out of the gate.

"Hey! Where are you going?" Fargo called after him, his voice low.

"I'll be back soon," Broken Oak said. Fargo watched as the old trader loped across the dark flatland and disappeared into a gully. If Crowheart were to spot the old man it would ruin everything, Fargo thought. Still, it was not likely that the renegade would be lurking around the fort before dawn. Still, he paced nervously for thirty minutes, his hand on the butt of his Colt, until he spotted Broken Oak returning. When he walked into the fort, Fargo saw that the blanket was slung over his back and puffed out. The old man went straight to the pit and emptied the blanket into it, shaking it violently. The he climbed wearily up the wall beside Fargo.

"Scorpions?" Fargo asked.

"Hundreds of them," the old trader said, removing the gloves. "With stingers."

They watched together as the east slowly lightened. As the sun rose, the others awoke, dressed, and ate quickly, then took their places. Broken Oak climbed down from the wall, fetched Fargo a full canteen, and positioned himself with Dade behind the barrels.

It was a long, hot day. They couldn't move around much or relax. Fargo, hunched down at the lookout, kept his eyes ranging over the dry, empty land, which remained still. The mules, hobbled in front of the fort, brayed occasionally.

Waiting, Fargo thought, as his tired eyes surveyed the land again, waiting was the hardest thing a man ever did. He pulled his hat brim down lower, deepening the shade beneath it. Far out on the flat, a silvery mirage, like a puddle of mercury, shimmered. And there, in the middle of the dazzling refracted light, Fargo thought he saw movement.

Just a flicker at first. He blinked his tired eyes and stared again, until he was sure. Yes, several black vertical lines danced in the center of the glittering lake.

"They're coming in," Fargo said to the others. There was a flurry of motion down below as they all jumped back into place, suddenly tense.

In a few more minutes, the bobbing black forms emerged from the mirage. They were still too far to count but it seemed like a half dozen or more. Fargo blinked his eyes again and saw only three. Three men coming on horses.

He moved so that he could look out the small rifle hole at the approaching men. He didn't want anything, not even the slight whisper of movement on top of the wall, to alarm them. When Crowheart saw the mules and horses hobbled in front, he would assume his own men were inside.

The three riders came on until Fargo could discern one in a red shirt and a black hat with a tall feather. He leapt down from the wall and slipped between the wooden gate, which stood open, and the interior wall. He drew his Colt and held it against his chest. After a long moment, Fargo felt the pounding of hooves through the earth. In another moment, he heard the creak of saddles and the jangle of spurs.

The three men galloped through the gate and reined in. Fargo could see them through a crack in the door. They dismounted swiftly. Crowheart called out in Apache dialect. When there was no answer, he drew his gun and looked at the other two. Crowheart gave a swift order and the three of them approached the pit. At the bottom was a blanket bundle, made to look like Conrad. The time had come to move. At Fargo's first shot, they would all fire.

Fargo silently stepped out from behind the door and raised the Colt, aiming it at Crowheart's red shirt. Suddenly, his attention was drawn by movement behind the barrels. Broken Oak had raised himself and was signaling something desperately to Fargo, pointing and waving and shaking his head in animated excitement. The old trader was so distraught Fargo couldn't make out what he meant. There was no time to lose. As the seconds passed, one of the three would suspect that something was wrong.

Fargo fired and the bullet caught Crowheart in the shoulder blade and spun him about, off balance. He dropped his pistol and waved his arms in the air wildly as he teetered at the edge of the pit and then fell in screaming. Dade and Tommy Gibbons fired as well. One renegade clutched his belly and crumpled immediately. The second, plugged in the leg, pulled up his rifle and returned fire toward the wagon. Fargo pulled up the Colt and shot the man in the neck. He went down heavily.

From the pit came the sounds of Crowheart's shrieks. Fargo knew that his bullet had not killed the famous renegade and that he was now being stung by the scorpions. He dashed forward and peered down.

Crowheart was writhing on the bones. One of his legs lay at an odd angle, broken in the fall no doubt, and he was covered with the scorpions. For a moment, Fargo considered putting the man out of his misery, but the moment passed. Broken Oak darted out from cover. The trader was so worked up he could barely get the words out.

"That ... that is not my brother!" he gasped, gesticulating wildly at the pit.

From behind, in the direction of the gate, Fargo suddenly heard the click of a trigger.

"Drop it! Both of you," a voice said. Fargo turned slowly and saw, standing in the open gate, four huge Indians. Their faces were scarred and hard as stone, their eyes darkly intent. All four of them had their rifles aimed straight at Fargo.

No way he could outshoot all four of them, Fargo thought. And they were standing in the doorway, where Dade, who was off to the side, didn't have a straight shot. Fargo tossed the Colt to the ground, not far from his feet. Broken Oak muttered a Cheyenne curse and threw down his rifle.

"Kick them."

Fargo did and then stared at the renegade who had spoken. He realized that he was finally looking at the real Crowheart. He and three more of his men had probably ridden down into a gully and crept up after the first three had come into the fort. Crowheart had ridden away from the campsite the day before with only two men. Fargo cursed himself for not suspecting that Crowheart had more men hiding out around Rio Chingo.

Crowheart's gash of a mouth had a cruel curl. His broken nose made him look like a hawk. His long hair hung loose over his thick, corded neck and powerful shoulders. His eyes glittered with something like greed or glee.

"So, my half-breed brother, the white man's slave," Crowheart spat, not moving from the doorway. "Your little bitch of a daughter ..."

But Crowheart got no further. At the mention of Summer Lightning, Broken Oak let loose a cry of rage and barreled forward toward Crowheart, who pulled up his rifle and fired. The old trader spun about, clutching his side, and fell heavily. Fargo kept his eyes on Crowheart, but he noticed that the old trader, as he lay in the dust, was still breathing and his eyes were squeezed shut in pain. Then the trader's eyes opened slowly and focused on his own rifle, which lay within a foot of his reach. Fargo did not let his eyes flicker toward Broken Oak, but continued to stare down Crowheart.

"Where's the girl?" Crowheart asked. "I was bringing her back to her father. Who says Crowheart is cruel?" He laughed, then sobered. "Now, where is she?" Now was the time to lure them fully inside, thought Fargo. Well into range of Dade and Tommy. In answer, Fargo shrugged, but he let his eyes dart toward the barracks.

"In there," Crowheart said triumphantly. His three men moved toward the low building just as the old trader's hand darted out for his rifle. Broken Oak grasped the gun and rolled over, firing up at Crowheart.

At the same instant, as the three Indians crossed the yard, gunfire exploded from the wagon and from behind the barrels. One of the renegades dropped to his knees and the other two sprinted for cover behind some empty crates. Bullets flew and ricocheted all around the enclosure as Dade and Tommy returned the renegade's gunfire.

Crowheart, hit by Broken Oak's bullet, jolted back, grasped his arm, and dropped his rifle. Broken Oak's rifle jammed and he crawled beneath a wagon to safety, his shirt wet with blood from his wounded side.

Fargo dove for his Colt, landing on the ground bellyfirst and sliding toward it through the dust. Crowheart, with a cry of rage, ran toward him. Fargo saw the kick coming and he raised his arms to protect his head, then thrust upward at the last instant, catching Crowheart's ankle and throwing him off balance. The Indian fell on top of Fargo and they rolled over and over, struggling.

Crowheart was as strong as an ox, Fargo found as he grappled for a hold on him. They stopped with Fargo on top, inches from the pit. The Indian's powerful hands closed about Fargo's wrists as he tried to force Fargo's arms upward. Fargo bore down with his sinewy muscles, feeling his bullet wound scream with pain. Crowheart's left shoulder had a fresh bullet in it, too, and Fargo jammed his strength into his left side, trying to break the Indian's hold. Sweat popped out on Crowheart's brow as his arms slowly sank back toward the ground.

Then suddenly, he jerked upward, freeing his left and thrusting it upward to Fargo's wounded shoulder.

Fargo was thrown backward by the impact and one leg dangled in space, over the scorpion pit. Crowheart threw himself upon Fargo and they scrambled at the edge, landing hard punches.

All around them, bullets whined and Fargo smelled smoke and heard the crackle of fire. He was nose to nose with Crowheart now, the Indian atop him as Fargo struggled to get his arms free again, inches from the pit. Fargo felt himself tiring, his left shoulder a fiery mass of pain. Crowheart, as if reading his thoughts, bared his teeth in a death's head grin. Fargo heaved upward, freeing his arms, and suddenly, there was a knife in Crowheart's right hand.

The shining blade plunged downward at Fargo's broad chest. He caught Crowheart's wrist just as the tip touched his shirt. Fargo summoned all his strength and their two fists trembled violently as they fought over the knife.

Fargo felt a black fury course through his body. It was hatred for all the horror Crowheart had brought, for killing Summer Lightning, torturing the major, and for the hundreds of brutal murders he'd committed over the years. Fargo's strength poured into his right arm like molten metal and Crowheart's hand, holding the knife, raised slowly, inch by inch. Fargo turned the blade, his muscles bulging with the effort, until the razor sharp edge was toward Crowheart's neck. Still the knife moved upward, toward the renegade's throat. Then, suddenly, there was a shriek and Fargo felt a jolt along his body, as Broken Oak hit them suddenly. With his dying strength, the old trader had barreled across the open yard toward them.

Crowheart was knocked off Fargo and he tumbled, head over heels, disappearing into the pit. Fargo grabbed at Broken Oak, who rolled toward the hole. He caught him by the collar and hauled him out.

Fargo peered down and saw that Crowheart lay across the other renegade. Crowheart was still, his head at an odd angle. His neck had been broken in the fall. The infamous renegade, the scourge of the Southwest, lay broken on a pile of human bones. Scorpions were already crawling over his body.

Fargo turned his attention back to Broken Oak. The old man lay panting on his side. He was bleeding badly.

"I'm done for," he muttered. "Leave me here. Get out. The gunpowder. The fire."

Fargo looked around. The other renegades lay dead in the yard. Tommy Gibbons, limping and bleeding, was climbing out of the wagon and Dade was going to meet him. Smoke was pouring out of the barrack. The gunfire had started a fire. Katie emerged, coughing and leading her father. Fargo glanced at the old trader and saw that the man was dying.

"Go well," he said to the old man. Fargo stood. "Get the hell out of here!" he yelled to the others. "That gunpowder's going to blow!"

Dade and Tommy made for the door and Fargo

helped Katie pull the major out the gate. As they emerged, Fargo pulled the throwing knife from his ankle holster. Dade and Tommy were already cutting the hobbles from the mules. The flames were high over the fort now and a pillar of black smoke rose hundreds of feet into the air. Fargo got Katie and her father on horses and drove them away from the fort as he continued to loosen the mules and shout to get them moving away from danger.

He sliced through the rawhide hobble on the Ovaro's forelegs just as the first gunpowder exploded with a roar. The impact threw Fargo against the horse's flank and he grabbed the saddle horn. The pinto trotted away from the fort, dragging him along through a hail of burning rubbish falling from the sky. Fargo pulled himself onto the pinto's back just as the second explosion rocked the earth, sending up a roar of orange fire. The Ovaro galloped straight away from the fort, following the pack of mules and horses which were running ahead.

Fargo reined in at the edge of an arroyo. Katie Conrad sat looking back at the fort, now a bonfire of leaping flames and billowing smoke. Major Conrad sat nearby on his horse, looking unconcernedly in another direction, his eyes vacant. Katie noticed Fargo's gaze.

"He may never get better," Katie said. "But at least he's not suffering anymore. How ... how can I thank you?"

Fargo smiled.

"I like adventure, too," she said with a smile, her eyebrows raised.

Then she turned her horse and rode toward the

others. The major noticed her going and spurred his horse to follow, his expression blank. Fargo followed her as well.

There weren't many women around like Katie Conrad, he thought. And it would be a long, slow journey back.

LOOKING FORWARD!
The following is the opening section from the next novel in the exciting *Trailsman* series from Signet:

THE TRAILSMAN #152
PRAIRIE FIRE

1860, the vast Plains ...
where savage men and savage beasts
made life a living hell

The last thing a man expects to hear when he is in the middle of a vast plain, surrounded on all sides by a sea of shimmering grass, is the merry tinkle of female laughter. Yet that is exactly what Skye Fargo heard as he rode slowly westward, and the instant he did, he reined up and looked around. The sound had faded, and Fargo wondered if his ears were playing tricks on him. Then it was repeated.

Puzzled, the big man guided his pinto stallion to the northwest, in the direction of the mirth. The presence of a woman was a mystery he couldn't ignore, especially since he was so far off the beaten track it was doubtful any other whites had ever visited the region before, except maybe for a few buffalo hunters.

Indians were another matter. Both the Sioux and the Cheyenne hunted buffalo there regularly. Occasionally the Arapaho did the same. But they never brought their women along, as far as Fargo knew.

A gap in the waving grass appeared, a break that told Fargo there was a gully ahead. Stopping, he ground-hitched the Ovaro and shucked his Sharps from its saddle scabbard, then inserted a cartridge and warily advanced. He had no idea what he would run into, but it never paid to take anything for granted when out in the wild.

The breeze carried voices to Fargo's ears. A man spoke first, a woman answered.

"—finally alone, I have something I want to say."

"Don't spoil it, Jeems."

"You know how much I want you, Flora. You're on my mind every bleeding minute of the day, from the time I wake up until I fall asleep."

"Did you hear yourself?" the woman responded testily. "You want me. You don't love me. I doubt you even care for me all that much. All I am is convenient."

"Don't be like this. Here, luv. Give us a kiss."

There was a rustling noise, followed by a loud slap. Fargo came to the rim of the gully and hunkered down in the high grass to see what was going on. The clipped accents of the speakers had added to his perplexity, but they in no way prepared him for the surprise he felt on seeing the struggling pair below.

A pert redhead whose long hair was up in a bun was fighting off the amorous advances of a stocky man sporting a thin mustache and a neatly trimmed goatee. It wasn't the style of their hair that was so surprising, rather the way in which they were dressed.

The woman had on a uniform of some sort consisting of a starched white blouse with frills at the front and a knee-length black skirt that flared at the bottom. She also wore black hose and, of all thing, dainty shoes with incredibly high heels.

Not to be outdone, the man had on a fancy three-piece black suit and shoes that were polished so highly they gleamed in the sunlight. A white shirt and black cravat completed his wardrobe.

Fargo could scarcely credit his own eyes. Here He was, in the middle of the vast prairie, in the heart of Indian country, and he'd stumbled on two fools dressed in their Sunday-go-to-meeting clothes. He didn't know what to make of it, but he did know how to react to the plight the woman faced. Standing, he stepped to the edge of the slope, trained the Sharps on Fancy Suit, and said matter-of-factly, "I'd get off the lady right quick, mister, unless you're partial to the idea of having your backside blown clean off."

At the first syllable the man glanced up, turned beet red, and jumped to his feet. He seemed about to say something until he realized the Sharps was trained on his midsection.

The woman rose slowly, brushing grass and dirt from her skirt. She cocked her pretty head and regarded Fargo quizzically. "You don't look like the knight in shining armor type, but I reckon a girl has to make do in a pinch." Her red lips curled upward. "Flora Livingstone at your service, big man."

"Skye Fargo."

"Do you live hereabouts?"

Fargo had to laugh. "Lady, do you have any idea where the hell you are?"

Her smile broadened. "If you ask me, I'm in hell. Although I'm a bit put out that they got it all wrong. Instead of fire and brimstone, there's nothing but this bloody grass."

Keeping the rifle fixed on the livid man, Fargo walked to the bottom of the gully and openly admired her curvaceous figure. "From where I'm standing, it looks as if I've found me a slice of heaven on earth."

Flora chuckled, her green eyes narrowing. "Aren't you the brazen one. I don't know whether to be flattered or upset. Could it be I've gone from the fire into the frying pan?"

"I don't force myself on women," Fargo said sternly.

She pursed her mouth a moment. "No, I don't suppose you would have to. I bet a handsome man like you has to fight the ladies off with a broom."

Her attention strayed to her companion. "You're lucky this gentleman came along when he did, Jeems. If you'd persisted, I would have seen fit to tell the earl."

"You bloody bitch—" Jeems growled, and got no further.

Skye Fargo took a single stride and rammed the stock of his rifle into the man's stomach. Jeems doubled over, sputtering, and stumbled to one side. A second blow, delivered to his temple, felled him in his tracks.

"My word!" Flora declared. "Did you have to do that?"

"He needs to learn some manners," Fargo said, and was flabbergasted when she threw back her head and brayed like a mule. "What did I say?"

"Manners are what Jeems is all about." Flora adjusted her blouse and gave the unconscious man a nudge with her toe. "He's one of the earl's two manservants."

"Who is this earl you keep talking about?"

"Perhaps you'd like to meet him? If you'd like, you can escort us back to camp."

"I'll escort you," Fargo corrected her. "Your friend can lie there and rot for all I care."

"Outspoken soul, aren't you?"

"I don't believe in beating around the bush, if that's what you mean," Fargo said. He nodded at the rim. "Let me fetch my horse, and we'll go see this earl."

"I'm at your disposal, kind sir," Flora responded, a devilish twinkle lighting her eyes.

Fargo knew an invite when he heard one. He climbed out of the gully marveling at the odd whim of fate that had resulted in the encounter. It had been a spell since he had last shared a bed with a woman, and the thought of Flora's ample bosom and shapely legs were enough to make his manhood as stiff as a board. He held the Sharps in the crook of his left elbow, took the pinto's reins in his other hand, and ambled back.

Flora was waiting at the crest. "Are you sure it's safe to leave poor Jeems here?" she inquired. "We heard such awful tales about red savages and all kinds of fierce beasts that roam this terrible prairie, although we have yet to see any."

"Count yourself lucky," Fargo said. He spied a thin gray wisp of smoke rising to the northeast and pointed. "Is that your camp?"

"Must be. I'm afraid my sense of direction is all askew out here, but they did have a fire going when I went for my stroll."

Fargo led off, aware of her studying him intently. "What are you folks doing in this territory?"

"We're on a hunting expedition. The earl goes on one at least once a year. Africa, India, South America, I've been to all those places with him." Flora sighed wearily. "He must have the world's biggest collection of stuffed heads. Tigers, lions, elephants, rhinos, you name it, he has one hanging somewhere in his castle."

Fargo glanced at her to see if she was joking and found she was serious. "What are you, his maid?"

"Goodness gracious, no. I work for the countess, his wife. The salt of the earth, that sweet woman is. Too bad she didn't marry someone with a better temperament."

"You don't like the earl much, do you?"

"Let's just say that if I didn't think so highly of her nibs, I'd be back in England right this minute enjoying a cup of tea and some biscuits while reading the London *Times*," Flora said wistfully.

Although it wasn't Fargo's nature to pry, he wanted to learn a little more before meeting the distinguished couple. "Where are you headed?"

"I honestly don't know. Hadden isn't one to announce his intentions in advance."

"Hadden? Who is he?"

"I'm sorry. Ashley Hadden is the Earl of Somerset. Kendra, my mistress, is the Countess of Somerset. I've been in her employ going on five years now." Flora paused. "Sometimes it seems a lot longer."

"How many are there in your party?"

"All told, twenty-one."

The total was a lot higher than Fargo had guessed, and he was about to ask why there were so many when the patter of onrushing footsteps to his rear warned him that the one called Jeems had recovered much sooner than he had anticipated. He whirled, or tried to. Iron arms looped around his waist, and he was bodily lifted and slammed to the ground, losing his grip on the Sharps. He felt Jeems pounce on his back and winced when a knee gouged into his spine.

"Jeems!" Flora cried. "Stop!"

The enraged Englishman ignored her. Fists flailing, he pounded away at the back of Fargo's head. Fargo absorbed several blows before he could bunch his leg and stomach muscles and heave. Jeems tumbled but rolled with the agility of an acrobat into a crouch. He aimed a vicious kick at Fargo's face, which Fargo evaded by jerking aside.

Shoving upright, Fargo barely had time to set himself before the manservant was on him again. This time Jeems assumed a boxing posture and flicked his left fist. Fargo blocked with a forearm, pivoted, and delivered a right to the gut that sent Jeems staggering.

Fargo tried to close in to finish Jeems off, but the man recovered swiftly. Rock-hard knuckles grazed Fargo's chin, and a follow-through clipped Fargo's cheek. Back-pedaling, Fargo traded punches, waiting for an opening he could exploit. It became apparent that Jeems was a skillful boxer, not one to make an obvious mistake. Fargo found it difficult to keep the slightly smaller man at bay.

From far away came shouts, signifying the people at the camp had observed the fight and were hurrying to the scene.

Flora was bellowing in unladylike fashion for Jeems to cease and desist.

Fargo shut both out of his mind and concentrated

on the matter at hand. He had been in more than his share of saloon brawls and could hold his own against almost anyone in a rough and tumble fight. But Jeems was a pugilist, a man who took his fisticuffs seriously, and now that his initial rage had subsided, he was circling Fargo, keeping out of reach while awaiting his chance to strike. Fargo couldn't simply charge, swinging wildly. He had to take his time, whittle his foe down.

Jeems tried a jab to the face that Fargo tipped aside. Pivoting, Fargo flicked a straight left at the manservant, and when Jeems elevated an arm to counter the blow, Fargo delivered a sweeping hook to the body that jolted Jeems from head to toe.

The Englishman backed off, scowling.

Suddenly Flora stepped between them and tried to give Jeems a shove. "Enough of this nonsense! Be civil, you brute!"

In response Jeems pushed her so hard she stumbled into Fargo, who had to catch her to keep her from falling. The momentary distraction proved costly, as Jeems leaped in and connected with a punch to the head.

Dazed, Fargo got clear of Flora and set himself. Jeems attacked, pumping his arms, trying to overcome Fargo with a flurry of punches, but Fargo held his ground and landed several solid hits. Again they separated, Jeems breathing heavily.

To the northeast arose the thud of hoofbeats as riders approached at a gallop.

Fargo didn't dare take his eyes off the manservant to see who was coming. He stepped to his right, his fists clenched and ready. Jeems foolishly slid in close, feinted, and attempted to plant an uppercut on Fargo's jaw, but he was so obvious that Fargo was able to glide inside the uppercut and rock the Englishmen with a combination. Jeems tottered, his arms drooping.

Drawing back his right arm, Fargo swung a roundhouse that toppled the manservant like a poled ox. The crunch of his knuckles on the man's mouth was as sweet as music. Fargo stood over Jeems, waiting to learn if another punch was necessary. Except for the flutter of eyelids, Jeems was still.

"You were magnificent!" Flora breathed.

Fargo glanced at her. "A five-year-old Sioux would be tougher than this joker."

The drumming of hoofs was almost upon them. Fargo turned at the same moment the foremost rider launched himself into the air. He glimpsed a sinewy man dressed in a brown suit, and then he was bowled over and the newcomer was striving to bash his brains in with the butt of a small pistol.

Only Fargo's lightning reflexes saved him. He dodged the first few blows, hooked his hands under the man's legs, and heaved. The man went flying. Fargo surged erect, saw the man sit up and go to level the pistol.

Without a moment's hesitation Fargo streaked his right hand to his Colt and cleared the six-shooter in a blur. The revolver boomed, the slug ripping into the man's shoulder and flattening him in the grass.

Whirling, Fargo confronted a half-dozen men on horseback who were slowing and in the act of un-limbering their hardware. "Do it and you're dead!" he warned.

Flora uttered a terrified shriek. Dashing forward, frantically waving her arms, she screeched, "No! No! Put down your guns! You don't understand! He wasn't attacking us!"

A tall man in an immaculate suit and derby hat paused with a revolver half drawn from a shoulder holster. He stared at Jeems, then at the redhead. "I demand an immediate explanation, Miss Living-stone. I distinctly saw this ruffian in buckskins as-saulting Mr. Jeems."

"It wasn't that way at all, sir," Flora said timidly. "Jeems attacked him after he stopped Jeems"—she froze and gave a little cough—"that is, after they had a minor disagreement."

"What was the nature of this disagreement?"

"It was nothing, sir, truly."

Fargo detected an underlying hint of fear in her voice and wondered why she didn't come right out and reveal the truth. He scanned the other riders to make sure none were trying to get a bead on him, then checked on the man he had shot, who was sitting up with a hand clasped to his wounded wing.

The tall man wasn't satisfied with Flora's answer. "Jeems is out cold and Oakley is sitting there with a bullet hole in him and you say it was over nothing?" His tone hardened. "You will provide more details, Miss Livingstone, this instant!"

"I'd rather not, Earl."

So this was the nobleman? Fargo mused. He studied Ashley Hadden and did not like what he saw. Hadden's features were flinty, almost cruel, his eyes smoldering pools of arrogance. He had a tilt to his head, as if he was looking down his nose at the whole world. And when Hadden spoke, he did so in a dictatorial way.

Right at the moment the earl's face was a marble mask of anger. "I will not tolerate insubordinate behavior, especially not in the hired help. You will account for your actions, please, and be quick about it, or I'll have you dismissed and sent back to England."

Her lower lip quivering, Flora said softly, "Jeems was having a go at me when this man came along and stopped him."

"Having a go?" Hadden repeated, blanching. "Am I to understand he was forcing himself on you?"

Flora replied in a strained whisper. "Yes, sir."

The earl's lips parted, exposing a neat row of small white teeth. "You swear this is the truth?"

"By all that is holy, yes sir, I do."

The look that Hadden gave Jeems did not bode well for the manservant. "Mr. Moulton and Mr. Heath, I want the two of you to take Mr. Jeems back to camp. He is to be confined to his tent until I send for him."

"Yes, sir," said one of the men addressed, a beefy man with enormous sideburns.

Hadden focused on the wounded man. "Are you in much pain, Mr. Oakley?"

"Not much to speak of, governor." Oakley slowly stood. "It's nothing compared to the time that bloody Zulu put a spear into me." His right arm tucked to his side, he picked up his pistol with his other hand, then scrutinized Skye Fargo. "Never saw anyone as fast as you before, son. You could have killed me if you'd wanted to, couldn't you?"

"Yes," Fargo admitted.

"Well then, I owe you my life. And I'm terribly sorry about the misunderstanding. I thought Miss Livingstone was in danger and acted without learning the facts first. My sincere apologies."

Fargo didn't quite know what to say. In all his wide-flung travels he'd never met anyone so outrageously polite. He'd shot the man, yet there Oakley stood smiling and offering an apology for the inconvenience!

The Earl of Somerset moved closer. "You will accompany us back to camp also, stranger, and give your account of the incident. When I'm satisfied that all the facts are known, you'll be free to leave."

Fargo couldn't resist a smirk as he stared up at the haughty noblemen. "I've got news for you,

Hadden. I'm not going anywhere with you. The only fact worth mentioning is that I'm leaving. *Adios*." He slid the Colt into its holster, turned, and gripped the saddle horn.

"I insist that you come with us," the earl snapped.

"I don't work for you," Fargo responded, mounting. "So I do as I damn well please." He touched the brim of his hat to Flora and was set to ride off when the sight of another rider approaching rooted him in place.

The rider was another woman, but what a woman! Fargo had seldom seen anyone so exquisitely lovely. She had lustrous blond hair that cascaded over her shoulders in golden waves. Her eyes were a piercing green, her skin as smooth as the finest silk. Every feature was so perfectly sculpted, she seemed more like a work of art than a living, breathing human being. Her vibrant body was clothed in a full-length gown that clung to her sensuous limbs, accenting her feminine charms. Fargo gazed on her and felt his mouth go dry.

Reining up, the blonde glanced at Hadden, then at Fargo. She blinked, as if in surprise, and seemed to make an effort to compose herself. "Would someone kindly tell me what is going on?" she asked in a musical voice.

"There's been a row, Kendra," Hadden answered. "It's nothing to bother your dainty head about, darling."

The Countess of Somerset's jaw twitched ever

so slightly. "Why not let me be the judge of that, husband? My dainty head has handled crises before. And since from the look of things Flora is involved, I have every right to be privy to whatever has happened."

"It's nothing I can't handle," the earl said with an angry edge. He nodded at Fargo. "I simply have to convince this rotter that it's in his best interests to visit our camp and provide his version of events."

Kendra Hadden looked at Skye. "Is there a reason you won't grace us with your company, sir?"

"My handle is Fargo. Skye Fargo. And the reason is that uppity so-and-so sitting next to you, ma'am."

Sparkling laughter burst from the lady's rosy lips. She caught herself, grinned at her simmering husband, and bestowed a ravishing smile on Fargo. "Yes, Ashley does have a flair for antagonizing people. But I wish you would reconsider."

"I'm on my way to Denver," Fargo said lamely. Inwardly he wanted nothing more than a chance to get to know this delightful beauty better, but his common sense told him that he was asking for a heap of trouble if he didn't curb his yearning.

"Surely Denver can wait a day or two?" Kendra countered. "We haven't seen a new face in ages, and we would welcome the chance to show what gracious hosts we can be."

Fargo couldn't imagine the earl as a gracious host

under any circumstances, but he hesitated, tempted by her beauty.

"We would be most grateful."

The Earl of Somerset chose that moment to interject a comment. "If this blighter doesn't want to honor our simple request, let him go on his way. Who needs him?"

"We do," Kendra said. "If we're to ever find our way back to civilization."

"You're lost?" Fargo asked in amazement.

"Sort of," Kendra replied.

"Didn't you hire a guide?"

"Sort of," she said again.

Hadden made a gesture of impatience. "We can handle our problems without this plainsman's help." He began to wheel his mount.

"No, we can't." Kendra stood her ground. There was a heartfelt appeal in her eyes, and a hint of something else, as she said, "Please, Mr. Fargo."

Against his better judgment, and although he had an inkling of what he was letting himself in for, Skye Fargo said, "Lead the way, ma'am." He lifted the reins and hoped he wouldn't live to regret his decision.